"What's the get-up gift, Cousin Seatta?"

"That a gift we born wid, come down from elders. You got it too."

"I got it too?" Angie grinned.

"Shoo!" Cousin Seatta snapped her fingers. "You got it jus like me an' yo mama. When I got problems, the get-up gift send me seein dreams. I can see me doin my best, things that astound the world. And when I'm doin' my best, a feelin come over me. Ooh, I feel right warm and bright all over myself. I call it the shimmershine feelin."

Other Bullseye Books you will enjoy

Getting Even by Mavis Jukes
Maudie and Me and the Dirty Book by Betty Miles
The Real Me by Betty Miles
There's a Boy in the Girls' Bathroom
  by Louis Sachar
What It's All About by Norma Klein

The Shimmershine Queens

CAMILLE YARBROUGH

BULLSEYE BOOKS • ALFRED A. KNOPF
NEW YORK

This book is dedicated to
Alice Childress
who gave me strength
and understanding

It is not our task as adults to show our young people
which road to travel in this life. Just give them the
light of knowledge and they will find their own way.

PROFESSOR JOHN H. CLARK

Chapter One

"Seems like this elevator is always breaking down," Angie Peterson complained as she pushed open the first-floor stairwell door in the lobby of the building where she lived. "Seems like I always have to walk up these stairs." Angie's slender, dark brown, ten-year-old legs stamped as she climbed.

"I got me a new rhyme," she bragged out loud, reciting her poem as she stepped.

> *"One, two, three, four, five, six, seven, eight*
> *Peep around the corner*
> *See who's there.*
> *One, two, three, four, five, six, seven, eight*
> *Might be a mugger*
> *waitin' on the stair.*
> *One, two, three, four, five, six, seven, eight*
> *Peep around the corner*
> *before I go.*
> *One, two, three, four, five, six, seven, eight*

Can't even trust
somebody I know.
One, two, three, four, five, six, seven, eight
Peep around the corner
Check out the stair.
One, two, three, four, five, six, seven, eight
Say 'Have a good day'
to the boogaman covered with hair."

"This is too serious," Angie complimented herself again as she arrived at the fourth-floor landing and opened the door to the hall.

> *"Open the door*
> *Look down the hall*
> *throw sumpum at the spiderman*
> *hangin on the wall."*

"It's silly," she laughed. "Yeah, I'm gonna tell Michelle."

Angie walked quickly to the apartment where she lived with her mother and two younger sisters. "I got to remember it . . . 'Peep around the . . .'" She repeated the rhyme as she opened the safety pin in the pocket of her summer jacket, took off the key, opened the apartment door, and went inside.

Angie's mother, Amanda Peterson, was sitting on the front-room couch, holding three-month-old Patrice. Great Cousin Seatta, visiting from Atlanta, was sitting on the couch too, talking with Mrs. Moore who lived across the hall.

They all nodded their smiled greetings to Angie's

"Hi, Mama, Cousin Seatta, Mrs. Moore. I'm fine." Angie smiled back, kissing Mama and Cousin Seatta, then giggled as little sister Lavenia got up from her seat in front of the television set and ran to her.

She grabbed Angie around the waist and hung there, making Angie do the monster walk down the hall and into the bedroom they shared.

"Go on, girl!" Angie freed herself from the three-year-old's spider arms and legs. Then, just as she did every day after school, Angie took off her book bag, collected her poem book and romance magazine, went down the hall and into the bathroom, and locked the door.

Away from her little sister, away from her mother and the new baby, away from her neighbor, even away from sweet Cousin Seatta, away from everything else in the world, Angie leaned her back against the locked door, closed her eyes, took a deep breath, and by the time she let the breath whoosh back out of her mouth, she was dreaming dreams.

After that, it seemed like her body didn't have any bones in it at all. She slid down the door to sit on the side of the bathtub, moving slow and smooth like floating on a cloud, still dreaming. This was her dreaming room. This was her dreaming time.

First, Angie dreamed herself back in her classroom at school, calling to the teacher, "Me! Me! Call me! I know the answer!" The rest of the kids clapped for her, backed her up. "Angie, you sure are smart," they encouraged her.

And she dreamed herself grown up too, with a good job and nice clothes. In her dream one day, she came

9

home from work and told her mother, "Don't worry, Mama, I'll pay the rent this month. And I'm gonna buy you a house so you won't have to worry no more and I'll pay for the food so you won't have to go show your face to those ol' food stamp people no more." And she dreamed her daddy was home again, telling her stories about when he was a little boy in Alabama.

Then Angie read one of the stories in her romance magazine and saw herself in the story wearing makeup, and her hair was real long and light colored, blowing in the wind. Then she dreamed, "What is my first boyfriend gonna look like?" She dreamed him too fine, nice, bragging on her all the time. "My beautiful Angie." He kissed her. "I love you, Angie." "I love you," she told him. They got married.

After that Angie dreamed she was a soap opera queen living in a big house in Hollywood, and she was an Olympic track runner too, showing plenty teeth and holding up her gold medals for winning first prizes. And she traveled all around the world helping people, making them happy. That's when the warm feeling came and Angie felt she was shining all over like the sun. Seemed like the whole dreaming room was shining, and in golden rhythms Angie stretched her arms toward the ceiling and swung them in different directions at the same time, like a two-propeller airplane taking off. She lifted her knees to her chest as if she was a bird walking, shook her hands in front of her, in back of her, quivered her hips and shoulders, rolled her head, hopped on one foot, then the other, crossed them, turned slow and deep low, and then . . . Mama knocked on the door. In her golden feeling Angela always forgot and made too much noise dancing.

"Angela! What are you doin in there?" Mama called. "I know you not goin to the bathroom makin all that noise. Come out of there right now, you betta. Cousin Seatta has to use the bathroom."

"I'm comin right now, Mama," Angie answered, as usual.

When she came out and went into her bedroom, and sat down to write her new poem in her poem book, she still had the golden feeling. Even when she did her homework later that night, it was easy. Seemed like her mind and her books and papers and pencil were all warm and shiny too.

Later that evening, as she washed out Great Cousin Seatta's comb and brush under the hot water in the bathroom sink, Angie said to herself, "When Great Cousin Seatta looks at you, she looks at you for real. She don't look at you the way lots of people look at each other. Her eyes don't slide off to the side like she tryin to hide sumpum she don't want nobody to know, sumpum like bein scared. Most people scared." Angie nodded, agreeing with herself. "You can tell by they eyes." She remembered how scared her father's eyes had looked that night last winter when he left to go live someplace else. "How come his eyes changed to scared?" Angie wondered, pausing with her hands submerged in the soapy water. "Used to see some 'I love me some little Angie' and 'I love me some Mama' in his eyes. Especially when he was tellin one of those ol' snake stories his father told him when he was a little boy, or when he put on one of his music tapes and told

11

Mama, 'Let's dance, baby. Harlem Cold Baloney! Get down!' Wasn't no scared eyes then, and when they played 'Ain't No Sunshine' and 'Lean on Me.' And when they slow danced and looked at each other for a long time, wasn't no scared eyes no place. Where they come from?"

Angie let the soapy water run out of the sink and turned on the rinse water. She couldn't remember when they stopped having their dancing nights or when the fussing nights started, but she remembered that she and little Lavenia were sitting on the couch in the front room one night and how she couldn't move and didn't know what to do or what to say when Mama and Daddy started fussing so bad. And how Daddy turned around and looked at her and Lavenia. That's when she saw "Daddy got scared eyes." She remembered how deep his voice was when he said, "What you lookin at?" And how slow he walked when he went into their bedroom and closed the door. Later, when he came out, he had his coat and hat on and his big suitcase. He didn't say anything, just went out. Went someplace else to live. Mama was standing there in the middle of the floor. She had scared eyes too. And later, when they were in bed, Angie and Lavenia heard Mama crying in her bedroom. Lavenia began crying too and got out of her bed and went into Mama's room. But Angie remembered that she couldn't cry or move. Even in the dark she could still see Daddy and Mama's scared eyes. When sleep came to her, it was almost time to get up and go to school.

Angie swished the comb and brush around in the soapy water. "I ain't never seen Cousin Seatta's eyes look scared," Angie thought, pausing. "She ain't scared of nothin. Maybe 'cause she too old." Angie tapped the cleaned comb and brush on the side of the sink to dislodge any remaining drops of water. "Seem like she too old to be travelin 'round the country by herself, takin the no-frills flight all the way from Alabama to up here in New York to come see us. But she did. I love me some Cousin Seatta."

"Angie!" her mother called from the kitchen. "You better come in here!"

"I'm comin," Angie answered, and hurriedly dried the comb and brush on the towel and gave the sink a fast rinse with hot water.

"Hurry! Come get yours," Mama again urged from the kitchen.

"You betta, else I'm gonna eat it up," she heard Cousin Seatta threaten. Mama and Cousin Seatta were sitting at the table in the kitchen, eating ice cream, and Cousin Seatta pretended to reach out for Angie's ice cream dish just as Angie plopped down into the chair next to her and protected it with her arms.

"Cousin Seatta, you gon get fat," Angie playfully scolded, filling her mouth with ice cream.

"Not me," Cousin Seatta boasted. "Fat don't light on me, afred to. But it not afred of gettin on a young thang like you, Miss. Betta let me eat yours so Mr. Fat can't get you." Cousin Seatta reached for Angie's dish with her spoon.

"It's all gone," Angie mumbled, her mouth full and running. "If it's gon get me, it's gon get me." As soon as she said that, Angie remembered how her father was always saying it. She looked over at her mother sitting across the table from her. Just for a second her mother looked back at her, then got up and collected the three empty ice cream dishes and took them to the sink to wash. "I don't want to see you gulp your food down like that again. You hear me, Angie?"

"Yes, ma'am."

"Cousin Seatta can't stay up all night. You better start her hair. Her plane is real early in the mornin and we gotta leave on time, can't be gettin up late."

"Yes, ma'am."

Angie took the clean brush and comb out of her lap and walked around to the back of Cousin Seatta's chair. Brushing and braiding hair at bedtime was Angie's idea. She made up the job for herself so she could have a reason to be up with the older women at night and hear what they talked about. She combed and brushed Cousin Seatta's hair into four sections the way she liked it. Then Cousin Seatta twisted the hair in each section into one long twist, then twisted it again into a small ball. And those balls didn't come loose either, even when Cousin Seatta was sleeping. Angie was amazed. Cousin Seatta wouldn't explain, just said she had "glue in her fingertips."

When Cousin Seatta finished making the last little ball, she said, "Come 'round front of the chair so I can look at your face, Miss Angie."

Angie put the comb and brush on the table next to Mama, then sat down in the chair on the other side next to Cousin Seatta.

"Why you wanna look at my face, Cousin Seatta?"

Mama laughed and picked up the brush and started brushing her hair.

"How old are you, chile?" Cousin Seatta asked.

"I'm ten, almost 'leven."

"How old do you think I am, Miss?" Then, without waiting for an answer, Cousin Seatta boasted, "I'm ninety years old."

"Ooh, Cousin Seatta, you ninety?"

Cousin Seatta laughed. "I got eighty years on you. How you gon catch up, Miss? How you gon catch up, Amanda?"

"How we gon catch up, Angie?" Mama laughed. "We put my years with your years"—Mama shook her head—"we still can't catch her, Angie."

"You got us, Cousin Seatta."

"When Cousin Seatta laugh," Angie thought, "she look like somebody else. Like she be laughin at a lot of things we don't even know about and like she ain't never gon stop laughin. She have a good time. Then she always come up with a surprise when she finish."

"You start dreamin yet?" Cousin Seatta asked.

"Dreamin?"

"Um hum. I dream all the time, Miss. When sumpum be worryin my mind, won't turn me loose. Sumpum secret I can't tell nobody, holdin me down, makin me all frowny-faced, that's when I start up a dreamin 'cause my get-up gift commence ta work."

"What's the get-up gift, Cousin Seatta?" Angie's eyes opened wide.

"That a gift we born wid, come down from elders. You got it too."

"I got it too?" Angie grinned.

"Shoo!" Cousin Seatta snapped her fingers. "You got it jus like me an' yo mama. When I got problems, the get-up gift send me seein dreams. And those sweet seein dreams lift up my mind till I can see all kinda different ways to lift my own self up from under whatever be worryin me. I can see in the future. I can see in the past. I can see me doin my best, things that astound the world." Cousin Seatta extended her arms out to the right and left of her, as if holding up the globe. Her voice trembled with awe at what she saw herself doing. "And when I'm doin my best, a feelin come over me. Ooh, I feel right warm and bright all over myself. I call it the shimmershine feelin."

"I get that feelin too. When I dream. You call it the shimmershine?"

"Yeah." Cousin Seatta squinched her eyes. "Got to give it respect. Give it a name. And when the shimmershine get on ya, everybody step back 'cause you commence ta work, work, work yo dreams till they comes real. Nobody can outdo you when yo get-up gift workin and you get the shimmershine. Yo worries don't mean nothin no mo. 'Cause yo get-up gift done took over. Amen." Cousin Seatta started laughing again. "Now, you say you dreamin?"

"Yes, ma'am."

"Then how come you still got the worried face? When I first come here to visit, I saw you was worryin 'bout sumpum. I didn't say nothin 'cause I figured soon 'nough yo get-up gift would start givin you seein dreams and by now yo worried face would be gone. But you still got it. Now dat means sumpum is pressin yo get-up gift down, keepin it from takin over. What pressin it down, Miss?"

"I don't know, Cousin Seatta, 'cause I'm dreamin.

16

And I get the shimmershine. My dreamin place is the bathroom 'cause it's quiet in there. I told my best friend Michelle and she got a dreamin place too. She tell me what she dream and I tell her what I dream."

"The bathroom." Mama nodded. "I knew you were doin sumpum in there beside what you supposed to."

Cousin Seatta shook her head. "Well, sumpum is wrong. What you dreamin 'bout?"

"I got a lotta dreams." Angie closed her eyes. "I dream I buy Mama a house. I put on makeup and everything and make my hair long and light colored like on TV. I dream I got a boyfriend and he real nice and we get married. And"—Angie lowered her voice—"I dream Daddy's home."

Cousin Seatta stretched out a long low "Uuum hum," looking at Mama. Her eyes seemed to open wider. "Yeah, those some nice dreams," she agreed. "An yo daddy is back home? I can see it too. But how come you dreamin you got long light-colored hair? Where you get dat dream from?"

"You know." Angie frowned. "'Cause it look better than my hair and my boyfriend like it like that. My hair is too short and it don't make me look right."

Cousin Seatta's eyes seemed to open even wider. "You got the color from the old country"—she stroked Angie's hair, then lifted her chin—"features too from Africa."

"From Africa?" Angie frowned.

"Yes. You a right good-lookin chile. Anybody ever tell you dat?"

"No, ma'am. You kiddin me," Angie moaned. "'Cept Mama and Daddy."

Cousin Seatta stretched another "Uuuum hum." "What people say 'bout yo looks, Miss?"

Angie almost stopped breathing. Suddenly she didn't want to be with the older women any longer. She wanted to be in bed sleeping. From across the table Mama was watching her. "Tell her, Angie," she coaxed.

Angie looked into Cousin Seatta's eyes. They were comforting and peaceful. She felt tears coming into her own. But she swallowed and blinked them back. Cousin Seatta had her hands folded on the table in front of her. With her middle finger Angie traced the bones and large veins through the dark skin on the back of her right hand and arm. "Sometimes people say mean things," she finally answered. "Say I'm too black, my hair is bad, call names."

Cousin Seatta nodded her aged head as if she knew what Angie was going to say before she said it.

"Girl, what you tell um when they say all that?" Mama frowned. "Callin you names? Who?"

"If one kid real dark, then the other kids laugh at the one that's real dark like me. Call all kinda names and stuff. Grown-ups do it too, just talkin about they don't like nothin too black. Talkin about black people ain't 'you know what.' I don't wanna say the word they say. If you tell um 'don't be sayin that,' they start fightin. I don't say nothin. I just look someplace else. I don't never look at um."

Mama stopped her combing. "Nothin? You don't say nothin? Angie, I don't want you to be fightin like those rough kids out there, but you have to stand up for yourself, talk up for yourself. Lookin down, that's

18

what your friend Michelle is always gettin on you about. You better stand up for yourself and look people in the eye. Talk up for yourself. Didn't we raise you to do that?"

"Yes, ma'am."

"Then why don't you?"

"What I'm supposed to say, Mama? I don't know why everybody's so mad at everybody." Angie folded her arms and leaned back in the chair. "Everybody got a attitude. They scared. Then they get mad and start actin stupid, fightin. I don't understand it. In that high school over on Wilson Street, two girls was fightin and one of um stabbed the other one and she died, and it wasn't about nothin. They was fightin about sumpum stupid. All them just scared. I don't look at um. I don't want um to see my eyes. You can see scared in people's eyes. Even Daddy had scared eyes when he went away."

Angie hadn't wanted to say what she had been thinking and feeling about Daddy going away. It just came out with the other things that had been worrying her.

"What you mean, 'Even Daddy'?" Mama leaned back in her chair with one hand on one hip.

Angie didn't want to answer her mother. "Cousin Seatta," she asked in a small voice, "you want me to turn down your bed covers and get your glass of teeth water for you?" It didn't work. Mama and Cousin Seatta waited. "Mama." Angie began to speak carefully, trying not to say anything that would upset her mother. But her words were like a troubled river surging from her mouth. "That night Daddy left, I saw his eyes was scared and he said he was gonna leave before he hit you. You and him was scared. Onliest difference was you didn't fight."

Angie couldn't hold back the tears this time. She slouched in her chair with her head down and they dripped from her cheeks onto her hands and terrycloth robe. Mama was sitting straight up in her chair now, her mouth and eyes open in surprise. "Baby," she moaned softly. "You been thinkin about all that?"

Cousin Seatta reached over and pulled Angie to her and put her arm around her, hugging her. "Ooh, we women gotta lot to talk about, don't we?" Then she turned to Mama. "Daughter, look like the chickens is finally out da coop. Worried face gon be gone soon."

Mama blinked her tears back. She couldn't say anything, just looked at Angie as Cousin Seatta wiped her eyes with a folded white handkerchief she had taken from the pocket of her robe. "Me and yo daddy"— Mama cleared her throat—"gon get back together. It's just gon take a little while. Angie, we love you and Lavenia and Patrice. It's just gon take us a little time. But we ain't gon be fightin and name-callin. And if somebody bother you, you come tell me or call and leave a message for yo daddy. You hear me, baby?"

"Yes, Mama." Angie sniffled as she walked out of Cousin Seatta's comforting arm and sat down again.

"With you seein and hearin all that, I guess you don't feel happy to be a black chile, do you?" Cousin Seatta shook her head in sadness.

"No, ma'am."

"Well, let's see if I can 'splain the story of dis fear and anger and fightin dat's worryin you so. You see, Angie, we grown-ups ain't been tellin you children what you need to know so da world makes sense to ya."

"Cousin Seatta, I tried," Mama started to explain, but Cousin Seatta put her hand up and stopped her.

"Amanda, I'm not pokin at you, daughter. You didn't get the story when you was comin up. 'Cause we ain't tellin. Dat's why our children runnin around crazy as bedbugs. 'Cause they don't know our story."

Angie put her elbows on the table and rested her chin in the palms of her hands. She wished her friend Michelle had stayed overnight at their house so she could tell about school too and hear what Cousin Seatta said the grown-ups weren't telling. Why didn't they tell? What did it have to do with the children being scared and calling names and fighting? Angie could tell there was something important and mysterious and frightening about it. She watched Cousin Seatta carefully as she sighed, then placed the palms of her hands flat on the table.

"Angie," she said, "a people's story is the anchor dat keeps um from driftin, it's the compass to show the way to go and it's a sail dat holds the power dat takes um forward. Now, the children is confused, going every which way, 'cause day don't have our story. Confusion make people scared and nervous and mean, make um feel bad about dayselves like you told us you and the children at school feels." Cousin Seatta coughed and cleared her throat.

"You'all want some water or tea or sumpum?" Mama asked, getting up from the table.

"Just water, darlin, um hum." Cousin Seatta nodded.

"Me too, Mama. Want me ta help ya?"

"Umph umph," Mama answered. Angie watched her take three glasses off the drying tray, set them on the sink, then go to the refrigerator for the plastic bottle of water. More than ever before, Angie liked being with the older women that night. Cousin Seatta had called her a woman. "We women have a lot to talk about." Angie recalled her words. She felt good. The feeling was almost like the shimmershine. "This is a special night," Angie thought, beginning to relax again. She watched her mother give them their cool full glasses and then sit down with her own.

Cousin Seatta drank slowly, then set the half-empty glass carefully onto the paper towel Mama had given them with their water. She made a smacking sound with her lips. "That's fine, daughter. Thank you. Now, Angie," she started the conversation again. "You was tellin us 'bout what goes on at school and what you see some grown folk doin. You 'spressed da opinion dat you feels uneasy bein a black chile. Am I statin what you 'spressed correctly?"

Angie was drinking her water as Cousin Seatta spoke. She drank all of it and placed her empty glass on her paper towel just as carefully as Cousin Seatta had. "Um hum." She nodded. "The other day at school, Hector come tellin me God made a mistake when He made our looks. Did God make a mistake?"

Mama "umphed" and sucked her teeth, and Cousin Seatta's chair made a creaking sound as she folded her arms and leaned back, scrunching up her face. "No, my sweet child—" She kind of sang the words slowly, spacing them out. "Aaand it hurts me to find out that our children is still talkin that kinda talk. No, God don't make no mistake. Take fa instance, the people what come from China got day kinda beauty look. The people what come from Europe got day kinda beauty look. The people what come from Africa got day kinda beauty look. Our people come from Africa so we got the African beauty look. And we just fine. All the looks is fine. Don't let nobody tell ya different." Cousin Seatta patted the table as she said each word. "Dat's God's work. If people was handing out looks, everybody would be a mess. Nobody wouldn't favor nothin. Day the ones that make mistakes. People who scared of other people. 'Day don't look like me,' day say. 'I don't look like dem. Day got more dan me. Day gon take away what I got,' day say. 'Fred day can't get what day want. Day 'freda da whole world but 'specially day own selves, and too 'fred to say it. So, ain't no pleasin um."

"Then they get mad. Right, Cousin Seatta?" Angie asked.

"You right. You smart too, not just good-lookin." Angie covered her face.

"Day get angry," Cousin Seatta went on, "and commence to do things to people what different from um. Just 'cause day different. Things day do so mean and chillin even God have to cry when He see it. So terrible ya can't let the thoughts of it rest in yo mind fa long." Cousin Seatta wiped her forehead as if wiping something from her mind. "Grown folk don wanna tell day children 'bout such meanness, it so bad." She rocked back and forth in her chair with her arms crossed, holding herself, looking straight ahead, seeing something long ago. Angie watched her, afraid.

"Don't get sick. You gettin sick? Mama, Cousin Seatta gettin sick?"

"You all right?" Mama asked.

"I'm fine, daughter." Cousin Seatta put her hand over her heart. "I'm still feelin the pain from when I was a chile. From the meanness I come up through. Das the kinda meanness put on our people. The wounds don't just go way on day own. We by rights must heal um." Under the table, Cousin Seatta's feet began to tap a quick rhythm on the floor. Angie had seen the elders do that in church when they were "moved by the Spirit." Mama stood up and went behind Cousin Seatta's chair. She rubbed her shoulders and held her head in her hands, resting it backwards just below her breast. "I think we should all go to bed now, Cousin Seatta. We wearin you out, we so glad to have you here."

"No, no." Cousin Seatta patted Mama's hands, taking them from her head and sitting straight up in her chair. "I'm fine. I can't stop now. Got to tell the chile. Can't let the chile go 'round with no anchor. I'm fine, daughter. Sit down, Angie, I'm just getting started. How 'bout you?"

"Just gettin started." Angie rubbed her hands, grinning. Under the table, Cousin Seatta's feet started tapping the floor again.

"Today is the chile of yesterday and da mother of tomorra. Fo all dat we know and do today, from yesterday we borra. Angie, European businessmens forced our people to come here from day homes in Africa, and made dem live here and work like day was slaves. Dat's how we got here. And day commenced to tell da

24

tale dat we didn't have no history back home, said we was savages. Said all da greatness came from day homes in Europe. But our people knew betta and resisted, so to make um as slaves day had to mess day minds up. We got plenty wounds come over from our slave yesterday. For near 'bout every minute of every hour of every day of every week of every month of every year fa mo dan four hundred years of slavery time, our people was pained, wounded, turned every way but loose, made to play da fool. Dat pain was part of the welcomin present for da new children born in all dem generations. Laws passed tellin us 'You can't learn to read, can't learn to write.' One slave lawmaker stood up in front of other no 'count lawmakers and tell um, 'We have as far as possible closed every road by which light may enter day minds. Iffen we could put out day capacity to see da light our job would be completed, for den day would be like beasts in da fields!' Talkin about our people, Angie. And da hurt and confusion from dem times, from dem laws, is still with us today. Weighin us down. After we was set loose from da chains, was no time set aside fo us to be 'bout healin. We was huntin jobs dat paid us money fa our labor, tryin to get us some learnin. But da Ku Klux Klan was hangin and lashin and runnin us, keepin da fear goin. When I was a chile, down in Alabama, three months outta da year was all da schoolin allowed to black children. Time we shoulda been in school, we was made to be in the fields workin. And da old schoolhouse was a one-room sumpum with a pot-belly stove, didn't heat hardly at all. We was usin raggedy two-three times hand-me-down books, not enough to go 'round. And a slate to make our lessons on. Betta not be too smart. Betta not think much of yourself and 'spress yo pride outside da family, else ya get kilt or whupped. We was ignorant and scared. Made so by law and kept so by fear."

"You was scared?" Angie asked in surprise.

"Sho I was scared. Iffen you in danger, you best be scared."

"You still get scared?" Angie couldn't believe it.

"Sometimes."

"How come I don't see it in your eyes?"

" 'Cause I don't let Mr. Fear set down in me, take his shoes off, and make hisself to home. Every time he tries to take over, my get-up gift set on him, keep him under control. But I wasn't held back and hurt much as some. Some was hurt so bad day couldn't never truly use day get-up gift. Commenced to fear everything black, including day own self. Afraid and shame of day own color, day hair and features. Day culture. Take to actin like da ones what got power over dem, da slave-makin people. Takin to thinkin like um, talkin like um, tryin to look like um. Den before the power people ridicule um, day ridicule dayself. Before day get name-called by um, day name-call day own self. Before day get hit by um, day hit day own self. All dat started in slavery time. We can't keep it goin. We got to let it go. We got to remember da old ones, da first ones come off da slave ships from Africa, find out what day knew 'bout us dat kept um strong. Day had dem old rules. Praise da Lord, amen. Don't ya think so, Angie? Daughter?" Cousin Seatta smiled.

"Yes, ma'am." Angie nodded and Mama agreed.

"Now tell me sumpum, Miss. How much time you spend tendin to yo hair? I been lookin at it."

"I guess just a little bit." Angie groaned, covering her head with her hands, surprised again by Cousin Seatta's change of direction.

"I seen it a coupla times look like a chicken been scratchin in it. Ya hair is real tight curled. Dat's fine. Be proud of it. Yo skin is a lovely dark color. Dat's fine too. Be proud of it. Yo features is full. Dat's fine. Be proud of um. And yo mind is good. Be proud of it. If you not proud of yoself, you can't dream reality, thinkin proud, seeing dreams. Instead, you'll have po little cloud dreams, floatin and driftin 'round bumpin into each other, goin nowhere special. Angie, dat's what happens iffen you stay 'fred alla time. Afred to do dis, do dat. Ya be like a shriveled-up-inside, don't-go-nowhere, do-nothin dead thing. Don't care 'bout nothin, nobody. Yo shine go out and da world hardly see you. Then when ya pass on out dis world, it be like you never was here. And dat's da worse thing could happen to yo life, my sweet child. Does dat make sense to ya?"

"Um hum, I understand." Angie nodded.

"Close yo eyes and set this picture in ya mind."

Angie and Mama closed their eyes.

"In dat powerful time when day was set loose from the chains of slavery, our people craved schoolin. Right away day went to work, buildin up schools fa dayselves. And wherever day heard tell of a school set up fa dem, day come from miles 'round to get in. Day come before work, after work, girls and boys yo age, Angie, mamas and daddies like yo's, grands, even

27

great-grands like me, come ahurryin. Some maimed or blind, with da rough swollen stripes from da whip and da dent from da chains still achin day bodies. Some didn't have no shoes and day clothes was raggedy. Day come by foots, mules, horses, buckboards, buggies, whatever would get um dere. And wasn't nary a bench or chair, beam or ledge in da schoolhouses what didn't have one of our people's bottoms settin on it. And every standin space was stood in. Day gloried in learnin. Respected it. And 'cause of day learnin, day families and our people did better fa dayselves. Can ya see dat picture, Angie? Amanda?"

"I can see it." Angie's eyes were still closed tight.

"I can too," Mama said.

"Open yo eyes. It was da get-up gift what brought um dere. Made um go to school," Cousin Seatta whispered. "'Cause da get-up gift raise itself up on knowledge. It shine on knowledge. Dat's what gives you da shimmershine dat lasts. So now, what you gon do, Miss Angie? Ya gon let fear and name-callin and da hate disease set on ya get-up gift and stop ya from doin ya best?"

"No, Cousin Seatta."

"Ya got ya task. I know ya gon glory in knowledge. Ya gon be a shinin chile. It ain't gon be easy, but it's gon be grand."

"Yes, ma'am. And I'm gonna tell my friend Michelle all about it."

Cousin Seatta's eyes were tired and her voice had quieted to a deep rich whisper. She held Angie's hands with both of hers. Angie didn't want her to ever let go and wondered if she would see her again after this visit.

"Now, Miss—" Cousin Seatta released Angie's hands and, placing her own hands flat on the table, slowly pushed herself up out of the chair. "I'll tell you a little more after you turn down ma bed covers and get ma teeth water."

Mama took Cousin Seatta's arm and helped her into the bedroom.

Chapter Two

The next morning, when she was dressing for school, Angie took special care fixing her hair and felt proud when Cousin Seatta and Mama and even little Lavenia told her how nice it looked. She had wanted to go to the airport with them, but Mama told her, "No, the subway might be slow or somethin, and you'll be late gettin back for school."

So she hugged and kissed Cousin Seatta, and said good-bye. After they had gone, she ate her breakfast, then went to the living-room window. Looking down at the walkway in front of the building, she saw her friend Michelle sitting on one of the green benches near the sidewalk, waiting for her to come down and go to school. Angie was anxious to tell Michelle everything she had talked about with the older women the night before. She turned from the window and checked the kitchen to see that all the gas burners were turned off, then if all the lights were off in the apartment. After that, she slammed the front door locked and double-stepped it down the stairway through the lobby and outside to where Michelle was waiting for her.

"Guess what we got, 'Shell." She grinned, full-toothed. "We got African beauty." Angela didn't stop at the bench where Michelle was sitting, but with book bag bouncing skipped past her toward the sidewalk. "We got us some African beauty!"

"What?" Michelle was puzzled, watching her go by.

"We good-looking too," Angela called back, posing beauty-queen style at the curb.

Michelle rushed to catch her friend. "What happened? What you talkin about, girl?"

The traffic light was red, and Angie was at the corner waiting for it to change as Michelle caught up with her.

"I'm talkin about what we got, Michelle. We got a lotta stuff. Mama and Cousin Seatta told me all about it last night. And Cousin Seatta is awesome. She a monster she so smart."

"What she say? What she say, Angie?"

"She say we got us a gift called the get-up gift. Born with it. It like God or sumpum. Invisible. When we in trouble, our get-up gift come to our rescue. It make us dream seein dreams and the seein dreams help us to get up when we feelin bad, and do our best and then, guess what? That's when we get the shimmershine feelin. You know how we felt when we was practicin on our poems for the block party?"

"I know I was scared. I didn't look at nobody when I was readin my poem. But we felt good, Angie. Our poems were fierce. I remember that feelin. Your mama was so happy she started cryin about your poem. We felt good. That's the shimmershine feelin?"

"Yeah, Cousin Seatta gave it that name, and we got it. Ain't that bad! Then Cousin Seatta said our dark color is good and our kinky hair is good. It's all right even if it's short. Just have to give it some respect, that's all. I feel like I got the shimmershine right now. Look at me, Michelle, am I shinin?"

Angie raced Michelle across the street to the block where the school was. When they reached the other side, she put her arm around Michelle's shoulder. "Mama told me I have to speak up for myself with people 'stead of lookin down and not sayin nothin all the time."

Michelle stopped walking. "I told you that," she complained, "but you didn't pay me no mind."

"Yeah, you did." Angie hugged her. "You my very best friend."

"You gon do it?"

"Yeah."

They walked on toward the school. "You already different."

"I got me a task I have to do, Michelle."

"What's a task?"

"It's a job. When Cousin Seatta was comin up, that's what they used to call it."

"You babysittin?"

"Unh huh."

"Well, what kinda job?"

"It's a task. Don't you be actin stupid when I tell you what it is."

"Girl, if you don't wanna tell me, OK. I mean, I thought we was friends. I tell you things. How come you so mysterious and stuff?"

Angie stopped walking and turned to Michelle. Her

33

arms were straight down by her sides and her head pushed forward and angled to the right. She spaced out her words. "I said I'm gon tell you."

Michelle stood her ground. With her arms folded, she patted her left foot and looked up to the sky with her head tilted to the right. She waited.

"My task is"—Angie continued in her pose and spaced her words even slower, not looking Michelle in the face—"I'm gonna glory in learnin."

Michelle slowly leaned back sideways against the school fence with her mouth open. "Huh?"

Turning quickly and with her head up, Angie sucked her teeth and proceeded to stamp her way down the sidewalk toward the school building. "You said you wasn't gonna laugh," she called back to Michelle.

"I'm not laughin. Serious. Tell me again. You gotta job in church?" Michelle asked, galloping to catch up with Angie as she stiff-legged her way through the schoolyard crowded with students and parents. At the brick steps on the right of the main entrance to the school, Angie stopped and sat down. Grinning and apologetic, Michelle sat next to her. "I was just playin. But I don't know what you was talkin about. For real."

"Michelle," Angie began slowly. "Kids can do things too. I mean they can help. Like, if I get real smart and learn a lot of good stuff and get me a good job, I can help my family. You know we don't have much money and stuff, and Mama and Daddy was always fussin 'cause of that. I think that's why he went away. Then, when he come back and I been studyin real hard and graduate and get me a good job, I can help out. That's why I told you I wanna glory in

34

learnin. 'Cause that's what the kids Cousin Seatta told me about did. And they helped their families."

"What kids?"

"The kids livin in the slavery time. Cousin Seatta said as long as the slave tradin was goin on, black kids couldn't go to school nowhere. They wanted to go real bad so when slavery time was over, a lot of um walked for miles and miles to get to school. Sometimes even through dark woods early in the morning or late at night, in the rain with no shoes on, just to get to school. Their mamas and daddies told them, 'You can't live good if you don't have knowledge.'"

"Knowledge?"

"Yeah. We have to know a lot of things, Cousin Seatta said, especially our story, our history. And they didn't have no big cities then. And most of the time all they had for breakfast was something called a hoecake."

Michelle leaned back against the building. "What's that?"

"I don't know." Angie shook her head. "Cousin Seatta told me that part when she was gettin in the bed and I didn't wanna ask her no more questions. She was too tired. But when they got to school, they was happy 'cause their minds was gettin food. When you hungry and you eat sumpum, you feel good. Well, their minds was feelin good 'cause they was eatin knowledge." Angie sat up very erect with her head high. "Cousin Seatta sat up like this when she tell me they gloried in learnin. So that's what I wanna do too."

"You mean you gon get down with the books?"

"Yeah."

"You gon shimmershine?"

"Give me five, best friend." Angie stood up and raised her hands to come down in the five.

"I wanna help my mama and grandmama too," Michelle said, standing up. "I wanna learn sumpum 'cause right now we ain't really doin nothin and I am bored. I wanna glory too."

"Yay!" Angie and Michelle began to dance. "We gon glory together." Angie grinned. "And we gon be fierce and fresh." Michelle clapped her hands. "We gon shimmershine so much the mayor won't have to turn on the streetlights. When we go someplace, people gonna come stand next to us so they can see. We gon be like streetlights."

Mr. Harvey, the school principal, came to the school doorway and began ushering in the parents and children who had gathered in the schoolyard. Angie and Michelle went in with the crowd, raising their voices to talk over the sounds of the activity that filled the first-floor hall.

Just before they reached the stairway on their way up to the third-floor class, Michelle asked Angie, "You know what you said about talkin up for yourself and not lookin down? You really gonna do it?"

"Yeah," Angie answered, climbing the stairs slowly.

"All right!" Michelle grinned and walked on ahead up the stairs with Nia.

"That's gonna be the hard part," Angie thought to herself. She had understood what Cousin Seatta told her about her color being good and her hair being good and how feeling bad about yourself can make you scary and angry and do mean things. "I understand all that, but I don't feel better yet. Maybe I'm

36

never gon feel better." Angie paused on the stairway. "I see grown-up people still feeling bad about theyselves."

"Daddy, sometimes in the summer when it's hot, people be goin off on each other like firecrackers," Angie had complained, wide-eyed. One night her friend Ann Marie's mother and father went outside to get some fresh air and were sitting on the steps in front of their building across the street. They were just talking. Something happened. Pow! They started to arguing and went off and broke on each other, fighting. And the people on the first floor, Mrs. Tatum. Her friend came to visit her and, pow! They went off on each other. Most of the time it was because somebody's feelings had been hurt or about money or sometimes even drugs. The ambulance was always coming. Angie remembered how every time that happened, Daddy would look sad and shake his head slowly. "People can't take but so much pressure," he would say. "Just so much."

On nights after Angie saw people go off, she would sit in the chair next to the window in the front room and look out up at the clouds and stars. She always felt better after she did that. And she felt comforted when she thought about Michelle. "She think more of herself than I think of myself. She don't let nobody mess over her. She look people in the eye and fight um too."

When Angie reached the third floor, Michelle was waiting for her. "You really gon do it? You not gonna be lookin down and stuff?" she asked.

"I told you I was," Angie assured her. "You gon help me?"

"Yeah, let's do this." The girls walked slowly down

the hall toward the classroom. "Every time kids start crackin on somebody," Michelle explained, "let's tell um what your cousin Seatta said about what the slave kids did and the get-up gift and all that."

"And where all the name-callin and talkin bad about theyselves come from. And its old-timey. Let's tell um that," Angie agreed.

The students filled the classroom by ones and twos, reluctantly, lingering just outside the door, then entering wearing expressions of boredom. Angie and Michelle went in with the other students, slowly taking their seats, Angie in the third row, third seat, and Michelle the fourth row, third seat. They were taking their homework from their book bags when Charlene, the girl at the desk on the other side of Angie, shouted, "Damn!" and slid down in her chair, glaring toward the teacher's desk. When Angie and Michelle looked to see why, they saw a white man who had just walked into the room standing behind the desk, trying to smile at the gathering students.

"We got a sub." Michelle sucked her teeth.

"I bet it's gonna be one of those days." Angie folded her arms and slumped in her seat. She sighed, watching the students react to the substitute teacher.

"Oh no, a sub," Cheryl complained, falling against the wall next to the door as she came into the room.

"Party time!" Darrell clapped his hands and grinned as he passed in front of the teacher's desk.

"I sure hope Darrell and Hector don't be playin 'round," Angie whispered, leaning her elbow on the desk and her chin in the palm of her hand.

"We don't do no work! We don't do no work!

Right, teacher?" Victor called from the back of the room. "We don't do no work when the subs come. No way!"

"All right! All right! Settle down!" The substitute teacher raised his hands to calm the class. When everyone was seated, he continued. "My name is Mr. Bonner. I will be your teacher for today."

Charlene moaned and put her head down on her desk. "I'm goin to sleep."

The girl in the seat in front of Angie's stood up. "Teacher, after this period we have an assembly, then we go home 'cause we only got half a day today. You know that?"

"Yes, I know it. Thank you. Your Mrs. Cooper left an assignment for you. I will write it on the blackboard for you to copy and follow." He reached into desk drawers, searching for chalk.

"Teacher! Teacher!" Hector and Darrell stood next to their seats in the back of the room, waving their hands.

"Here it comes." Michelle scrunched up her face.

Mr. Bonner's eyes were nervous. He pointed to Hector. "Yes?"

"Teacher!" Hector looked as though he were in deep thought. "Augh! Augh!"

Charlene, Cheryl, and Pat began imitating Hector's "Augh, aughs" and watching Mr. Bonner for his reaction.

"Hector, sit down," Michelle called back to him.

"Yes, sit down." Mr. Bonner glared at Hector as he found the chalk and turned to write the assignment on the blackboard. Angie, Michelle, Juan, and Nia began opening their composition books.

"Mr. Bonner! Mr. Bonner!" Now Darrell, waving his hand, called from the back of the room.

Mr. Bonner turned quickly and glared at him, then at the other students who were laughing behind their hands.

In frustration, Angie pressed her fingers into the shallow scratches on the desktop. "I wanna do my task," she moaned. Then she stood up and repeated as loud as she could, "Teacher, I wanna do my task!" All eyes were on her.

"You buggin out?" Charlene asked.

"She breakin." Cheryl, whose seat was in front of Angie, leaned away from her. "Teacher, put her outta the room."

"I want you to do your task too." Mr. Bonner nodded, turning to write the assignment on the board.

"Yo, you!" Darrell called again, walking down the aisle. "I raised my hand. You didn't call on me. What's the matter, Mr. Bonner? I'm not gonna do what Hector did. He retarded. He just twelve. I'm thirteen. I'm a man. Yo. You gon answer my question?" Darrell had walked halfway down the aisle as he talked.

Mr. Bonner continued to write out the assignment on the board. "Wait just a minute," he called back to Darrell over his shoulder. Angie sat down. She, Michelle, and some of the other students began to copy down the assignment in their composition books. Other students, led by Charlene, encouraged Darrell, who stood in the aisle mocking Mr. Bonner behind his back. When the assignment was on the board, Mr. Bonner put the chalk on the rim of the board, brushed off his hands, and turned to face the class. Darrell was standing next to his desk, wearing his most innocent face.

"What do you want? What is your name?"

"Darrell," Charlene, Hector, and Cheryl called out. Darrell bowed.

"What do you want, Darrell?"

Michelle slid down in her seat and slowly spaced out her words. "Don't do it, Darrell."

"Do it!" Charlene and Cheryl hollered, glaring at Michelle.

Mr. Bonner glared at them, then quickly looked back at Darrell, who was now standing even closer to his desk.

"Go back to your seat, Darrell. When you get there, I'll answer your question."

Darrell didn't move. "Yo, man. I wanna make a deal with you. Since you a sub, I don't think we should do no work. Like, you don't know what we been doin."

"Your teacher left an assignment. It is on the board. Get to work. Now!" Mr. Bonner spoke crisply, his arms folded over his chest.

Darrell stared at him, at his eyes, at his clothes. "But she not here. We should be playin games, man." Darrell did a dance step and as he turned, his outstretched hand knocked Mr. Bonner's papers and books off the desk and scattered them onto the floor. Some students "oohed" and covered their faces with their hands. Others laughed and clapped. Angie and Michelle folded their arms and complained, "This is dumb. We just wastin time."

As Cheryl ran up to Mr. Bonner's desk, shouting, Darrell climbed on top of it and started the moon walk. Other students began running around the room.

"Get down off that desk," Mr. Bonner shouted and bent down to pick up his scattered books and papers from under the feet of the taunting students.

Michelle walked quickly up to the desk and pushed Darrell off. "Get on down from there," she shouted. "Why you gotta be so stupid?" Then, turning to Charlene, "This is dumb. Why you always gotta do this kinda stuff?"

"Leave Darrell alone!" Charlene shouted back, glaring at Michelle from a distance. "He can do what he wanna do! You gon tell everybody what to do?"

"I don't have to take this," Mr. Bonner shouted, putting his papers back on the desk. "Get back in your seats."

"Oh yeah, we gon get you fired. You ain't never gonna work again!" Darrell hollered. Angie put her head down on her desk and covered her ears, but sat up again when the room suddenly became silent and Michelle nudged her in the side. She looked up to see Mr. Tucker, the black teacher from across the hall, standing in the doorway.

"Uh oh." Angie sat back in her seat. "They gon get it now. Mr. Tucker don't play."

On top of the desk Darrell quickly stopped his dance and stood still, looking at Mr. Tucker, waiting for him to make his move. Charlene, Cheryl, Pat, and Hector had seen him before Darrell and hurried to their seats.

Mr. Bonner turned to see what had caused the action to stop. Without taking his eyes from Darrell, Mr. Tucker came into the room and extended his hand to Mr. Bonner, who shook it. Darrell slowly climbed down from the desk and with just a hint of a boasting dip in his walk returned to his seat. The room was silent. Then Mr. Bonner picked up the papers he had missed before and the book from under the desk. Angie and Michelle and most of the students were pleased that Mr. Tucker had come.

"I hope he put um out of school," Michelle whispered just loud enough for Cheryl and Charlene to hear. Angie looked at her with big eyes.

"Cheryl, Charlene, Pat, Darrell, Hector, you all know you are not supposed to bring that into the classroom, don't you?"

Angie looked from Mr. Tucker to the five accused ones, who all looked at Mr. Tucker as if they didn't know what he was talking about.

"Don't play that innocent stuff with me. I saw you through the window before I came in here. Stood out there for five minutes watching you disrespect the other students, your teacher and yourselves. Isn't that what you did?" Mr. Tucker's voice was low, his smile knowing.

Now, none of the accused looked at Mr. Tucker. They looked at the floor or at the ceiling.

"Isn't that what you did? Answer me. You better get real. You know I've had you suspended before. You don't wanna see me in the principal's office again, do you? Didn't you disrespect this class?"

"Yeah, yeah, yeah," they answered.

Mr. Tucker cupped his ear. "I didn't hear you. What did you say?"

"Get um, Mr. Tucker," Michelle sighed.

"Yes, Mr. Tucker," they all shouted.

"Sit up!"

The five shifted in their chairs, sucked their teeth quietly, rolled their eyes to the ceiling or down to the floor.

"Let me tell you this here." Mr. Tucker pointed both his forefingers at the five. "You come to school to learn. That's your job."

Angie grinned and nodded. "That's their task," she said quietly. But Mr. Tucker heard her.

"What did you say, Angela?"

Angie was startled. She hadn't meant for him to hear her. She spoke quietly. "I said, that's their task, Mr. Tucker."

"You're right, Angela. It doesn't matter if you have a sub or your regular teacher. It is your task, your job, to learn. And I'm talking to the whole class now. Don't let any student in your class or anybody else stop you from learning, from educating yourself. Don't fight it. Grab it. You five were fighting it." He pointed at the five. "Do you know why you were doing that? Don't sigh, look at the ceiling, and shuffle your feet. That's not an answer. Do any of you kids know why some of you act mean and nasty the way you were acting when I came in here? What about you, Angie?"

Angie looked at Michelle. She didn't want to draw any more attention to herself but she wanted to answer, to tell what Great Cousin Seatta had told her. "'Cause they don't have too much respect for theirselves," she finally answered.

"Aw, shut up!" Charlene turned around and glared. "You always tryin to bo be sumpum else, tryin to be so smart."

44

"Why shouldn't she try to be smart?" Mr. Tucker pointed his finger at Charlene. "*You* should try to be smart. Right, Mr. Bonner?"

Mr. Bonner was sitting at the desk again. He nodded.

"And you, Cheryl. And you, Pat and Darrell and Hector. All of you should try to be smart. Maybe you would find out that you are."

Mr. Tucker turned to Mr. Bonner and they talked quietly. Then he turned back to the class. "All right. You know I'm right across the hall. If I hear any more disturbance from you, you are going to be suspended if I have anything to do with it. And you know I do."

When Mr. Tucker was gone and the door was closed, Charlene, Cheryl, and Pat all turned to glare at Angie and Michelle, cutting and rolling their eyes at them.

"Finish your assignments," Mr. Bonner said from his seat. "You don't have much time, but do as much as you can." He folded his arms and watched them until the bell rang.

"We in trouble," Angie moaned, pulling her book bag on as she and Michelle walked down the stairs to the auditorium.

"I don't care about them," Michelle answered. "Nobody betta not come messin with me."

"But I did good, didn't I?" Angie questioned, looking for reassurance. "I talked up for myself."

"Girl, you hollered up for yourself!" Michelle laughed, patting Angie on the back. "'I wanna do my task—'" She imitated Angie's stiff-legged stance in the classroom. And with Angie laughing beside her, continued her jerky stiff-legged walk down the aisle in the

45

auditorium. "This the way you looked. 'I wanna do my task.'"

"I didn't know I was gonna holler. It just came out," Angie was finally able to say when she stopped laughing.

Without noticing them, Angie and Michelle had passed the cold stares of Charlene, Cheryl, and Pat, who had grouped themselves at the door, sure that they would be noticed.

"Tomorrow I'm gonna test my get-up gift again," Angie promised as they settled in their seats. "And I'm gonna shimmershine."

The next day was perfect for Angie to test her get-up gift. Their regular homeroom teacher, Mrs. Cooper, was back and the last subject of the day was Communication Arts. Each student would have to stand up and read two paragraphs from the reading assignment. The night before, Angie had practiced reading the assignment over and over, using her finger to follow the words. Then she closed her eyes and saw herself in the schoolroom reading out loud. She saw the other students cheering her and Michelle grinning. "The get-up gift is working." If only it would happen that way in class.

When it was time for Communication Arts, Angie and Michelle looked at each other, anticipating the coming challenge to Angie's get-up gift.

"I don't care what nobody say, I'm gon stand up and read, I'm gon read." Angie nodded, agreeing with herself. She sat up tall in her seat, her arms folded, her book open on the desk in front of her. Charlene and the gang had not said anything to them all day, only stared at them with blank eyes.

Just before the reading started, Michelle said, just loud enough for Charlene and her group to hear, "I sure hope everybody be cool. I'm gon be cool. If somebody start crackin on me, I'm gon tell um real nice, 'I'm tryin to learn sumpum, chill out.' But if they don't listen, I'm gon go upside their head."

Angie looked at her. "That keep it goin, 'Shell," she whispered.

Michelle opened her book to the assigned chapter. The first student in the first aisle stood up. Angie had two aisles and two students to wait before it was her turn to read. But as usual the cracking started as soon as the first student began.

"You can't read," Darrell taunted the student. "You should sit down and shut up."

Then Hector joined in. "Sound like she readin with her mama's teeth. You wearin yo mama's teeth?"

Mrs. Cooper warned them and they let the rest of the aisle read without commenting. They just sighed or shuffled their feet. But as soon as the first student in the next aisle stood up to read, "I can't hear her, teacher! Tell her to talk louder!" Hector shouted.

"I don't wanna listen to this." Darrell picked up his book and notebook and walked toward the door. Hector did the same.

"Sit down!" Mrs. Cooper commanded them. The two boys stopped at the door.

"But they can't read, Mrs. Cooper," Darrell shouted, turning back.

"I can so read," Natilee, the girl who had been interrupted, answered. "You two just didn't do your homework. You the ones can't read. That's why you tryin to get out the room."

Some of the other students applauded and laughed. Darrell did not like to be laughed at. He ran over to Natilee and pushed her down in her chair. "Shut up!"

"Sit down and stop this!" Mrs. Cooper shouted, coming around the desk and clapping her hands to stop the confrontation. "Sit down, Darrell and Hector."

Neither Angie nor Michelle watched them as they went back to their seats. They were both aware of something unusual. Charlene and her friends had not said a word during the outburst.

"They waiting for us." With every crack and outburst, Angie had become more tense. She kept her eyes on the page and when the reading resumed, read along with each child in turn. But when it was her time to read, Angie was afraid to stand. Mrs. Cooper had to call her name. She stood up slowly with her book open to the page but in her nervousness lost her paragraph. There wasn't a sound in the room. Finally she found her place. Angie put her finger under the first word and opened her mouth to read.

"Sit down, ugly!" Charlene turned around and shouted at her. Her friends and some of the other students laughed.

"You betta cool out," Michelle warned.

"Yeah, sit down, bitch!" Darrell hollered.

"You can't read nothin," Charlene continued, eyeing Michelle. "Yo lips is too big."

"Ain't nobody got big lips 'cept yo mama," Michelle hissed from her seat. "You betta be cool, Charlene."

"Don't be talking 'bout my mama!" Charlene jumped to her feet, glaring at Michelle.

"Stop it right now! Don't get crazy!" Mrs. Cooper stamped her feet and walked around to the front of her desk. "Sit down, Charlene, and be quiet. You too, Michelle." Charlene continued to stand. "Do you want to go to the principal's office? Do you want to have to bring your parents to school?"

"My parents ain't comin to this old school." Charlene spit the words out as she sat down, falling into her chair.

"Now let this be the end of it." Mrs. Cooper chopped the air with her hand as she spoke, then turned quickly and returned to sit at her desk. Angie was still standing in the aisle.

"Read, Angela." Mrs. Cooper hit the desk in exasperation.

Angie's hands were shaking. She closed the book. "We not supposed to call names and talk bad about each other," she said softly. "When you do that, it mean you don't have no self-respect. A lotta that came from long time ago when we was made slaves and treated so bad we started feelin shame in front of each other. Then the Ku Klux Klan was killin and shamin and we didn't have no laws to protect us and we lost a lotta respect for each other. But we don't mean it."

"Shit!" Cheryl threw her book on the floor and stood up, slamming her chair backwards into Angie's desk. "Yes, I do mean it too! You dumb and ugly! Teacher, she callin us slaves. Who she think she is? You oughta send her to the principal's office."

"Don't be callin me no slave," Charlene and Pat yelled. "You a slave."

"I'm just tryin to tell you we have to glory in learnin like the slave kids did and not be fussin all the time about nothin," Angie continued.

Mrs. Cooper pounded her fist on the desk. "Angela, will you please read! Or if you will not, sit down."

Darrell and Hector yelled from the back of the room, "Yeah, sit down! You can't read no way."

"Big lips." Cheryl cut her eyes at Angela.

"I'm gon read." Angie opened her book again and was finding her place when the bell rang.

"Don't move from your seats," Mrs. Cooper commanded the class. As she proceeded to give out the homework assignment, Darrell and Hector ran from the room. "I'm gone!" Darrell called back. "I'm history!" Hector slammed the door after himself.

"You did good," Michelle praised Angie. "You talked up."

"Next time I'm gon read too," Angie promised, walking down the aisle behind Michelle.

When they reached the door, Charlene, Cheryl, and Pat were standing just outside. As soon as Michelle entered the hall, they began to taunt. "Here come the slave kids." "Look like Africans." "Ugga bugga." "How come you tryin to go fa bad, Michelle? Better go over to Africa and be bad 'cause you ain't doodoo in this school," Charlene shouted, standing in Michelle's way.

"Don't pay her no mind," Angie cautioned Michelle, pulling her jacket sleeve, directing her to go away from them to the right. Michelle made cold eye contact with Charlene, then turned to go down the hall with Angie.

Natilee saw it first and screamed, "They gotta knife!"

Pat had begun to take the knife out of her jacket pocket but when Natilee screamed, she let it fall back into her pocket and walked down the hall and out into the schoolyard. When Michelle and Angie heard Natilee, they turned at once to face the gang of girls. Angie was closer to them but Michelle stepped between her and Charlene, who had already raised her hand to strike Angie. Charlene held her raised fist frozen in place above her head.

"Be a fool, Charlene. Go 'head," Michelle challenged her.

Charlene lowered her hand. She had seen Michelle fight earlier that year and remembered her thoughts at that time: "She a monster!"

"You think 'cause Angie is quiet alla time you can mess over her. Just 'cause she nice, you think she weak, so you gotta call people names and stuff. You just ignorant. Can't nobody tell you nothin. Well, let me see you run that shit on me. Come on, Rocky, you so bad, break on me. Come on!"

Michelle assumed a left-foot-forward battle position and with sudden and great speed pushed Charlene backwards onto Cheryl and Hector, who had come back to encourage the attack. Natilee had run into the classroom to tell Mrs. Cooper what was happening, and Mrs. Cooper came into the hall just as Michelle was pushing Charlene. At the top of her voice she yelled for them to "Stop that fighting! Michelle, I saw you!"

"She broke on me, Mrs. Cooper," Charlene explained. "I was tryin to walk down the hall and she come pushin on me."

Mrs. Cooper grabbed Michelle's arm and pushed her up against the wall. "You stay there. Everyone else leave this building."

"What you pickin on me for?" Michelle protested. "She started it."

"Shut up, Michelle! I saw you attack her. You're going to the principal's office."

"Yeah, take her to the principal's office," Charlene called back, and she and her gang walked down the hall and out of the building in triumph. Only Angie was left behind standing in the center of the hall. Everything had happened so fast. And now Michelle was blamed.

"Mrs. Cooper, Charlene started it. Michelle and me was walkin down the hall mindin our business. Michelle didn't start it," Angie pleaded for her friend. Mrs. Cooper wouldn't listen. With Angie just behind them, she directed a protesting Michelle down the hall to the principal's office.

"You not fair, Mrs. Cooper," Michelle complained. "You didn't do nothin to Charlene and the other kids. Charlene started it and the other kids was callin names and talkin mean and everything. You didn't bring um to the principal's office. You not fair."

"Fair smair, you hit, Michelle." Mrs. Cooper shook her finger in Michelle's face when they stopped in front of the office. "You are not supposed to hit people. You've done it before. Inside!" She motioned with her hand for Michelle to enter the office ahead of her. "Go! Right now. Explain yourself to Mr. Harney. Angela, you go home! Now!"

The Shimmershine Queens

"No, you didn't see it, Mrs. Cooper. Charlene and them had a knife. Michelle didn't start it. Why don't you listen? You didn't see it!" Angie and Michelle were both facing Mrs. Cooper just outside the door. Angie was holding on to the sleeve of Michelle's jacket and walking backwards into the hall.

"Angela! Let go of her arm and go out of here or I will call your mother too. Inside, Michelle! Right now!"

"Wait for me," Michelle murmured. She pulled her sleeve out of Angie's grasp and foot-dragged into the office, followed by Mrs. Cooper. "This is dumb."

"Ooh, Mrs. Cooper took Michelle to the principal's office, Angie?"

"Yeah." Angie turned to answer Natilee and Dawn, who had followed them down the hall.

"She not fair." Natilee shook her head. "She never do nothin to Charlene and them."

"Sure don't." Dawn scowled. "You gon wait for her?"

"Yeah." Angie turned and began walking slowly down the hall. "I'm gon wait outside."

"That's the wack," the girls agreed. "Dumb!" "Stupid!" they added, walking down the hall and out into the schoolyard. They separated at the fence, leaving Angie leaning against it, dejected. "See you, bye."

"Suppose Michelle get suspended," Angie thought. "And she didn't even do nothin." Suddenly, through the fence, someone pushed Angie and sent her sprawling forward onto the sidewalk, where she lay wide-eyed and stunned for a moment, then quickly scrambled to her feet. When she turned around to discover who had pushed her, she saw Charlene. Cheryl and Pat were with her.

"Angie, slave kid, how come you wrote this note to my boyfriend?" Charlene asked, waving a piece of paper in Angie's face.

Angie stared at her. "Charlene just wanna fight," she thought. "I didn't write no note."

Charlene punched Angie on the shoulder. "How come you write this note?"

"I didn't write no note to your boyfriend."

"Yes, you did! Didn't she, Cheryl? Didn't she, Pat?"

"You did write it." Cheryl punched Angie on the other shoulder, forcing her back onto a car parked at the curb. "Slave! I saw you."

"We saw you too," shouted Shawnell, a girl from another class. Pat backed her up. Angie sidestepped between Cheryl and Pat, and began to walk quickly down toward Amsterdam Avenue, but Charlene's gang quickly followed and surrounded her.

"You ain't goin nowhere. How come you ain't got no boyfriend of your own?" Charlene asked, punching Angie in the chest. "I know how come. You too ugly, that's how come."

Angie tried to continue walking but Charlene pulled her back and turned her around to face her.

"Charlene's boyfriend wouldn't even look at yo ugly black behind." They all laughed.

Pat started singing, "Ugly blue-black thing with kinky hair. Nobody want you and nobody care 'bout no blue-black thing with kinky hair."

Angie looked around at the faces of the girls as they laughed and punched her.

"How come you don't say nothin?" Charlene stood with her arms akimbo.

"'Cause she too dumb and ugly," Cheryl shouted, her face pushed up close to Angie's. "Callin somebody slaves. You the slave. You always tryin to be sumpum different. You ain't nothin. Then come writin a note to Charlene's boyfriend."

Angie reached for the note in Charlene's hand. "Let me see it. I can show you. It's not even my writing."

Charlene shoved her back onto the girls behind her.

"Don't be fallin on me!" they screamed. "Get off me!"

Other children began to gather around. "Fight!" they shouted. "Throw down!" The shouts grew in number and volume as from all directions children ran to form a crowd, then a screaming mob that surged and pushed till Charlene and her gang made a tight circle with Angie in the center. Angie looked around at the yelling children that pressed in on her.

"I'm not gon fight," Angie shouted at Charlene and her gang, then at the yelling mob.

Charlene pushed the crowd back. "Yes, you are!" she hollered back at Angie. "And don't be lookin for Michelle. I'll kick her ass too, if she come up here."

Angie tried to get away through the crowd, but no one would let her pass and Charlene pulled her back.

"Leave me alone, Charlene," Angie shouted. "I'm not gon fight," she started to say, but before she could finish the sentence, Charlene smacked the word "fight" out of her mouth and tears to her eyes. The crowd screamed louder.

"You ain't nothin. Your mama ain't nothin."

Angie stiffened. "Don't talk about my mama, Charlene."

"Yo mama get street-line food. You and her ain't nothin but dumb and ugly!" Charlene continued her taunt. The crowd screamed, "Ooh, she talkin 'bout Angie's mama. You gon let her do that, Angie? If she talked about my mama, I'd kick her ass."

"You black and ugly!"

"You black too. My cousin Seatta said it's all right to be black."

"I ain't as black as you. I don't look nothin like you. Yo old cousin don't know nothin. She ugly too."

The only face Angie could see now was Charlene's. It seemed as if the sky and the trees and the cars and the air were all screaming around her. Then Charlene's hands were reaching for her hair. She felt herself lunge at Charlene, clamping her hands in her hair, pulling it, twisting Charlene's head right and left, and right and left. Charlene's arms flailed, grabbed at Angie, as she tried to pull her head out of Angie's grasp, to pull away from her. The mob of screaming children scattered, running up and down the block, up on and between parked cars, but returned to crowd the two fighting girls. Whenever they could, Cheryl and Pat tried to hit Angie.

"You ugly, you ugly," Charlene continued to scream. Every time she heard those words, Angie jerked Charlene's head and shook her. Charlene fell. Angie straddled her, holding her down and twisting her own body from side to side to avoid Charlene's hands as they reached up to scratch her face. Cheryl pulled Angie's hair from behind and Angie felt kicks on her book bag and legs. She heard Cheryl's voice scream, "Get off her, ugly bitch."

Then someone from the crowd shouted close to her ear, "Pat got a knife!" Angie turned quickly, looked around for the knife. She tried to pull herself up off Charlene, who kept pulling her down, scratching at her face. Suddenly she felt herself being lifted up and out of Charlene's reach and set on her feet. She heard a woman's voice shouting, "Stop it! Go home!" Then a man's voice: "Back off! Get on out of here! Go on home like you got some sense."

The crowd began to open up, jumping and running. They continued to scream, "Fight!"

The man grabbed Charlene, trying to persuade her and the gang to leave and go home. They didn't listen but tried to get around him and at Angie.

Angie looked back and up at the woman who had pushed her way through the crowd and pulled her off Charlene. She was dark like Angie and wore oversize tortoiseshell glasses. Her eyes were open wide with the excitement of what was happening.

"Where do you live?" she asked. Angie couldn't speak but pointed to the building on the corner.

"Come on, I'll take you home," the woman said, putting her arm around Angie's shoulder. The mob of children had not broken up. They still surrounded Angie and the woman and the man, who continued to try to persuade Charlene and her gang to leave.

When Angie and the woman turned to go, Angie saw Michelle coming toward them through the crowd. Just at that moment Charlene and the gang broke away from the man and came running to Angie and the woman. The mob surged around them as Charlene ran around the woman to grab Angela. When she saw

Michelle, she stopped but it was too late. Michelle swung her arms in a furious motion, knocking Charlene backwards onto Cheryl and Pat and Dawn.

"Come on!" the woman shouted, pushing Angie and Michelle in front of her through the crowd that followed them for a short distance, then thinned and finally drifted away. Angie was limping. Her knees were scuffed and showed through her torn jeans. Her jacket and sweat shirt were torn and the barrettes were gone from her hair. Tears and mucus wet her face.

As they walked up the block to the apartment building, Angie felt Michelle take her hand and the woman lift her book bag off her back. Michelle kept asking her, "You all right?"

Angie didn't answer but just kept walking.

"Are you sisters?" the woman asked.

"No," Michelle told her. "We friends. We live in the same building."

"What's your name?" the woman asked Angie. Michelle looked at her. "She can't talk right now. Her name is Angie. My name is Michelle."

Inside the lobby of the building, Michelle told the woman, "The elevator is broke again. We got to walk up the stairs." She pushed open the stairway door and they went through and started to walk up the stairs. But Angie's legs had no strength. She couldn't climb the stairs. The woman helped her sit right where she was, in the middle of the stairway. "Take your time. Just rest a minute. I heard something about a knife. Did you get cut?"

Again Angie didn't answer. She was still breathing fast. Michelle looked inside her jacket and at her hands and neck. "Naw, she ain't cut."

"Is your mother home?" the woman asked.

"Yeah, her mama's home," Michelle answered, sitting down on the steps next to Angie.

"I don't wanna worry my mama," Angie began to sob. "She got problems."

"It wasn't none of your fault," Michelle tried to comfort her. "Charlene just crazy. I know she started it and I'm gon get her too. I'm gon tell your mama what happened. Don't worry. I'm gonna tell her for you."

"Well, Angie." The woman stood in front of Angie, took her hands in hers, and looked into her face. "I know your mother will understand. Don't worry, I'll talk to her and Michelle will too. Don't worry, you hear?"

"Yeah, it gon be all right," Michelle promised her, redoing the braids where the barrettes used to be. The woman dried Angie's face with a tissue.

"You feel better now? Want to try it again?"

Michelle helped Angie stand and the three slowly walked to the fourth floor.

Mama was sitting on the couch in the front room when they came in the door. She was talking on the phone but when she saw them, she forgot she was talking and began to shout, "What? What happened?" She didn't get up, just sat there with the phone in her hand, looking at Angie, who didn't move from where she was in front of the closed door.

"Mrs.—" The woman started to talk to Mama, then realized she didn't know her name.

"Mrs. Peterson," Michelle told her.

"Mrs. Peterson," the woman continued, "Angela was in a fight at school. But she's all right."

"A fight?" Mama said, still staring at Angie. The woman walked over to Mama and extended her hand. "I'm Ms. Collier. I'm a new teacher at Angie's school. I don't know the details but from what I saw, Angie was not the aggressor in the fight. And I think she's in pretty good shape."

Mama was still holding the telephone in her right hand. "I'll call you back," she told the person holding on and hung up. She took Ms. Collier's hand.

"I wanted to see that she got home safely and that you knew what happened."

"Thank you," Mama said, still looking at Angie.

"She didn't start it, Mrs. Peterson," Michelle explained. "It was that old stupid Charlene and her friends and them. They was mad 'cause Angie tried to tell um to stop callin names and crackin on everybody in class. And they had a knife too. I'm gon tell Mrs. Cooper and the principal about that. They always sayin they not doin nothin wrong."

"A knife?" Mama frowned. "Come here, baby—" She held out her arms to Angie. When Angie came to her, she examined her face, hair, arms, and legs. She turned her around, looking at her torn jacket and scraped knees. "Well, you not cut, just a little banged up. How you feel, baby? How you feel?"

Angie swallowed and nodded. "OK," she said softly. "I'm sorry."

"What you sorry for?"

"I didn't wanna fight." Angie's tears started again. "They made me. I tried to tell them what Great Cousin Seatta said but they wouldn't listen, Mama."

"Well, the devil with um." Mama frowned. "I told

you everybody not gon listen to what you tell um. But that don't give um no right to beat on you. I'm gon have to go to that school. This gon have to stop."

"Let me know if I can help you." Ms. Collier smiled at Mama, extending her hand again. "It was nice meeting you all. Sorry it had to be like this. Maybe I'll see you at school, Angie and Michelle?"

Mama stood up and took Ms. Collier's hand again. "Thank you." She smiled. "Excuse me for not getting up when you came in. I been feelin a little tired lately. Thank you for bringin Angie home. I thought you was they teacher." Mama began to walk Ms. Collier to the door.

"I might be soon," Ms. Collier said. "I'm teaching in a new program called Arts in Action. I teach drama and dance. It starts next week and if Angie wants to be part of it"—Ms. Collier looked back at Angie—"and if you want to be in the classes, Michelle, your teacher will have a form for your parents to sign. Get it signed and bring it back by Friday and the following week you start classes."

Angie brightened a bit. "You teach actin and dancin?" she asked.

"Yes, you like to dance and act?"

"They love it." Mrs. Peterson laughed. "I'll sign the paper."

"I'm gon go." Michelle walked to the door. "I'll call you tonight," she said from the hall. "We gon take actin and dancin, Angie. We gon be stars."

Angie watched Ms. Collier and Michelle walk down the hall to the stairway. Michelle stuck her head back out of the stairwell. "We gon be stars. See you."

When Angie closed the door, she turned to see that Mama had already lain down again on the couch. "You betta wash up and change ya clothes," Mama said quietly.

Angie walked over to her. "You depressed again, Mama?"

"You stop worryin about me, you hear? And stop apologizin for things. You didn't start the fight, and I know you been worryin about it, but you not the cause of the trouble me and your daddy havin. You not the cause of nothin bad. Sometimes people get confused like Cousin Seatta told us. They don't want the people who love um to see um humbled and feelin weak. Your daddy tryin to get hisself together and he forgot I'm his best friend, that's all. He can't see I'm on his side, can't see it. But we been married eleven years and we gon work it out. All this is hittin me kinda hard right now but I know we gon work it out. It's not yo fault."

Angie watched her mother's eyes fill with tears, saw how she couldn't say all that she wanted to say, and how deeply she sighed.

"I'm gon help you, Mama." Angie patted her mother's hand. "I'm gon be real good and real smart and get me a job so we can have some more money."

Mama began to shake her head. She covered her face with both hands as tears flowed through her fingers and down onto her neck. Angie ran to the bathroom and returned with a wet facecloth.

Mama cleared her throat and, taking the cloth from Angie, began to press it to her face and neck. "Mama's gonna be all right. I just need a little time. That was your daddy I was talkin to on the phone. You wash yourself up, change your clothes, then call him. Tell him what happened. Tell him you're all right. Tell him I'll talk to him later. Go 'head now. I feel better. If he's not there, leave a message."

Angie got up and slowly walked to her room. "You sure you all right now?" Mama called after her.

"Yes, ma'am."

Lavenia was asleep in their bedroom and Angie moved quietly. She picked up her pencil and poetry book and walked down the hall to the bathroom. When she leaned her back against the locked door and closed her eyes, took a deep breath and let it flow from her mouth, her body did not relax as it had always done before. Instead she felt stiff and brittle, like a piece of dry wood. She looked in the mirror at herself, examined the darkness of her skin, the fullness of her features, her short hair. She touched the tender, raised, red-edged outline of Charlene's hand that striped her left cheek. Tears began to come again to her eyes but Angie shook her head. "No! I'm not gonna cry. No more." Quickly she filled the sink with water and bent to press her face into it.

Later, when she called her father, it was hard to talk. After she told him about the fight, she could only tell him that she missed him and ask, "When you comin home?"

In her sleep that night, Angie was fighting with Charlene again. But Daddy was there too. Angie was running to him. "Daddy! Daddy!" she screamed. "I don't wanna be a firecracker! I don't wanna be a fire-cracker!" Then the light was on and Mama was sitting on her bed, shaking her, wiping the perspiration from her forehead.

"Wake up, Angie. Wake up. You not gonna be no firecracker. What firecracker? You're all right. You're my little girl. Firecracker?"

"Is Daddy here?"

"No, baby."

"Is he comin back, Mama? When's he comin back?"

Mama looked away from Angie. "I'm gonna talk to him, baby. Unh huh. Go to sleep."

Chapter Three

Mama usually had breakfast made by the time Angie got up in the morning. But when the alarm clock went off and Angie woke up, she didn't hear the sound of movement, nor was there the smell of food. Mama was still in bed, not asleep, just lying there. When she saw Angie peep into her room, she called, "Angie!"

"Yes, Mama." Angie walked over to the bed.

"You have to stay home from school, be Mama today, OK? I'm still a little tired."

Angie sat on the side of the bed and Mama held her hand. "How you feelin this mornin? Let me see your face. Look like it's gone down."

"I feel better, Mama. You want some breakfast?"

"No, but the baby's awake. You have to wash her, put clean clothes on her, and give her her formula. Is Lavenia still sleepin like a log?" Mama laughed.

Angie nodded her head, smiling. "Um hum. She don't wake up till she smell food."

"Well, get her breakfast too, but wait till you finish with Patrice."

Angie enjoyed playing Mama. After she had bathed, oiled, and dressed her, Angie kissed little Patrice. "You just a baby. Don't know nothin yet. Don't know how to talk up for yourself. You can learn, though, just like me." Angie laid the baby down on the couch in the front room and gave her her bottle. "Ain't nobody gon call you names neither. 'Cause I'll take care of you. And when you get to school, kids gonna know better."

When that was done, Angie thought about school. "Oh no. I'm gon miss the new teacher and won't get the paper for the dance class." She tore a page from her composition book and wrote a note to Michelle, asking her not to wait for her but to get her consent paper for the acting and dancing class. When it was time to meet Michelle, she called and waved to her from the window and dropped the note.

Later, when Mama was feeling better and it was time for school to let out, Angie asked Mama if it was all right for her to go meet Michelle at school. Mama said yes.

Angie hurried from the apartment and toward the school. When she walked into the school block, past the places where she had fought with Charlene the day before, she began to tremble again. The building across from the school had a low stone fence in front of it. Angie went there and sat down. Her knees were shaking and she was glad no one was there to see. "But I stood up for myself." Angie spoke out loud and it made her feel better. "I didn't let Mr. Fear make hisself at home in me. And they didn't beat me up like they wanted to. They so crazy. I bet they get-up gift ain't never gonna get up. Bet they ain't never gon shimmershine. Come upsettin Mama. She got enough problems. Don't need to be comin up to school 'cause a them. They not gon beat on me no more. I'm gon take care of myself."

The sound of the school bell interrupted Angie's conversation with herself. Almost immediately the front door opened and children ran out into the yard. Michelle was one of the first ones out. When she heard Angie calling from across the street, she ran over to her. "Girl, what happened to you?" Michelle asked. "Why you didn't come to school? You hurt from the fight?"

"Come on, I'll tell you," Angie answered, tight-lipped, walking off down toward Columbus Avenue.

"Angie, you think Charlene and her old friends gon bother you again? Unh huh, they scared."

Angie kept on walking.

"Angie, what's wrong? Why you actin like this? We best friends, right?"

"Right," Angie answered without breaking her stride.

"That book bag you got is just like mine? I told you when I got mine so you could ask your mother to get you one too. Right? 'Cause we best friends, right?"

"Yeah." Angie kept stepping.

"So tell me, best friend, why you didn't come to school? You sick? Where you goin?"

Angie stopped, took a deep breath, looked up to the sky, and shouted, "I got sumpum important to tell you. I'm goin to our bench in the park. Come on! You givin me stress!"

As soon as they arrived at the bench, Michelle sat down and folded her arms. "What?" she asked.

Angie slowly sat down, pushing herself backwards over the wooden slats. "My mama's sick. That's why I had to stay home."

"Aw, Angie, what's the matter?"

"She gets depressed sometimes. Now she feelin bad 'cause Daddy gone and she don't know when they gon get together. Sometimes she stay in bed all day, so that's when I stay home and take care of my little sisters. I didn't tell you before. I just didn't wanna talk about it. We got problems in our house."

"Did she go to the doctor?"

"Yeah, she goes to see the doctor but it don't look like it helpin."

"Maybe my mama can come over sometime and talk to her like she used to. She just been busy."

"Ask her to come, 'cause Mama don't go out and talk to people no more. Mrs. Moore from across the hall come over sometimes but most of the time Mama be cryin or sleepin. That's why I got to do real good in school so I can learn me sumpum and get a good job. I told her I was gon glory in learnin and get a good job and help her and Daddy. She got real happy."

"She gon be all right." Michelle put her arm around Angie's shoulder. "I'm gon tell Mama. She gon get better. I thought you was sick from the fight. I was plannin to tear Charlene and her gang up. All of um."

"Naw. Old Charlene betta not come tryin to beat on me no more."

"Aw naw, Angie." Michelle leaned back on the bench, laughing. "When you break on somebody you a monster. Natilee told me you tore her up. She said Pat, Cheryl, and Dawn was scared of you when you threw down on Charlene. You broke."

"I was scared too, 'Shell." Angie took a deep breath.

"But you didn't back off her. You took up for yoself. Give me five."

"Charlene talked about Mama and Cousin Seatta." Angie extended her hand for the five.

Michelle sucked her teeth. "How she gon talk about somebody?" She laughed. "That man that was tryin to stop the fight told that she started it and her mama had to come to school this morning. She was mad. She smacked Charlene right in front of Mrs. Cooper and everybody. Charlene started cryin. I didn't feel sorry for her. She always smackin somebody. But she didn't change. When Mrs. Cooper gave out the consent papers for the drama and dance class, she said, 'I don't wanna do no bugga bugga dancin.' Then threw her paper on the floor."

"She crazy." Angie stood up and the two girls began the walk to their apartment building. "Did you get the consent paper for me?"

"Yeah, I got one for you. We suppose to bring um back on Monday and we can take the class."

"We gon have dancin and actin too?"

"Yeah."

"What the teacher say we have to wear?"

"Wear what we got. Sweat pants or shorts or jeans. Wear what we got."

"Ooh, this is too sweet. I can wear my red sweat pants. Give me five, best friend."

The two girls walked into the building. "The elevator's workin." Angie clapped. Michelle pushed the button as Angie began to dance around.

"What kinda dancin we gon do?"

"I think African."

"African? We gon have drummin and everything?"

"Yeah, and we gon do a show."

The elevator door opened and they danced in. "A show?" Angie opened her eyes wide. "In the auditorium? With everybody lookin?"

"I know you gon show out." Michelle imitated Angie dancing. "Everybody gon see how good we are. They gon respect us. Serious, Angie. Guess what they gon call us?"

"What?"

"Angie, we gon be the shimmershine queens."

Angie screamed and squealed in delight as the elevator door opened and she ran dancing down the hall to her apartment.

Chapter Four

On Monday morning, Angie pulled her blue denim cap down over her ribbon-tied hair, leaving thin wisps of short straightened strands sticking out from beneath the sides and in the front. Excitement smiled in her eyes and it took her barely a minute on her way out of her bedroom to take her book bag off the doorknob where she hung it every night, stuff it with a stack of books from the small desk in the corner, and rush from her room, almost running, past the living room and kitchen area, down the short hall to the apartment door.

"Bye, Mama," she called out as she undid the locks and turned the knob to open the door.

"Wait. Angie, come in here," Mama called from her bedroom.

"Oh no, Mama," Angie groaned as she closed the door, turned with head to one side, shoulders drooping, and marched into her mother's bedroom. "You said you was feelin all right, Mama," she said softly.

Mama was dressing the baby on her bed as Lavenia watched her.

"I don't wanna be late. We gon have our first class with Ms. Collier," Angie pleaded.

"I'm sorry." Mama sighed. "You gotta stay home. The baby's sick. I have to take her to the clinic. You have to stay with Lavenia. You know I don't have no money to pay for no babysitter. I'm sorry. You know Michelle always tells you what happens in class when you have to stay home."

Angie couldn't believe it. "No, Mama," she moaned, louder than she had intended. Spinning around, she dropped her book bag on the floor and leaned against the wall by the door, stamping her feet. She didn't see her mother coming but suddenly Mama was standing over her. "Who are you talkin to, girl? You betta pick that book bag up! Don't you try it with me. Not this morning," Mama shouted as she picked the baby up off the bed and, with Lavenia behind her, hurried into the living room. Placing the baby on the couch, she made sure she couldn't fall off, then went into the kitchen area just off the living room. She turned one of the stove burners on, took a curling iron out of the kitchen-table drawer, and laid it in the flame.

In the bedroom Angie picked up her book bag by the strap and dragged it into the kitchen behind her. She stopped when she saw her mother sitting at the table. Slowly Angie walked to the window. Looking down to the street, she could see Michelle waiting for her to come down. Tears filled her eyes. She began to cry softly and bob up and down. Then, turning to look at her mother again, she said, "Mama, please can you take Lavenia with you?"

Mama was sitting quietly at the table looking into a small round mirror she had propped against the sugar bowl. After a moment she turned and lifted the hot curling iron from the stove in back of her and waved it in small circles, clicking the handle open and closed, cooling it. Then, catching a small section of hair in the iron, she began to make small tight curls.

Angie asked again, almost whispering, "Mama, can you take Lavenia with you?"

After another moment, Mama looked at her. "You say sumpum, Angie? Tell me what you said, baby. I wasn't listenin."

"I said, please can you take Lavenia with you?"

Mama looked at Angie for a long moment, then pressed the hot curling iron into the damp cloth and watched the cloth darken from the heat. "Come here, baby." She put the cloth and the hot iron down on the table and, in an effort to pull herself together, took a plastic comb from the drawer and fluffed up her hair. When Angie came to her side, she embraced her. "Give Mama a hug. You my big girl, Angie, right?"

"Yes, ma'am." Angie hugged her back.

"You have to help your mama today. Sometimes it's too much for me to carry the baby and be draggin Lavenia too. You know how they keep you waitin for hours in that clinic. Then Lavenia gets tired and starts showin her behind and gettin on my nerves, and I can't take it right now. So I have to depend on you to give me some help sometimes. Now, do what I ask you and don't give me no mouth this mornin."

Mama held Angie in her arms and they rocked for a minute. "No tears, you hear? Do what I ask you

73

now." Mama kissed Angie on top of her head. "Can you do that for me?"

Wiping away her tears, Angie smiled a delicate "Yes, ma'am."

Mama turned away from her and back to the mirror, checked her hair, and began to put the hot comb and other equipment away. Angie watched, then walked slowly over to the couch and sat down next to the sleeping baby. The child was still except for the shallow rise and fall of her tiny chest. Angie smoothed her bright yellow dress and freshly oiled hair. "Mama, baby sister got a fever."

Walking into the bedroom, Mama called back, "I know she got a fever. How come you think I'm takin her to the clinic? Leave her alone now before you wake her up. Where my keys? Find my keys for me."

Angie picked the keys up from the end table and took them to her mother as she sat on the bed, putting on her shoes. "Here they are, Mama. I found them for you."

Mama took the keys and put them in her purse. She was startled when the doorbell rang. On the couch in the living room, the baby jumped at the sound, cried out, then settled into sleep again.

Mama sat down heavily on the bed. "Angie, go tell Michelle you not goin to school. Now she done woke up the baby. Go tell her before she rings that bell again. She knows she not supposed to ring the bell in the morning."

Angela rushed to the door while Mama went to the baby on the couch, with Lavenia following behind. Angie looked through the peephole and opened the door. "It's Mrs. Moore, Mama," she called. "Hi, Mrs. Moore. I thought you was my friend Michelle."

Mama walked back into her bedroom. "Come on in here, Moore."

Angela let Mrs. Moore in, closed the door, then followed behind her.

"Brought you some sweet rolls to go with the coffee you gonna offer me." Mrs. Moore smiled as she entered the bedroom. "You feelin betta? Where you been hidin?"

"No coffee, no sweet rolls this morning. The baby's sick. I'm takin her to the clinic. I ain't much betta."

"Aw naw, girl, this ain't been no easy year for you. One thing after another. What's wrong with her?"

"I don't know. She got fever, throwin up, goin to the bathroom all night. Just went to sleep a little while ago. How come you home?"

"Started workin nights. But I'm not used to it. Can't sleep. Can I help you?"

"Yes," Angie answered from the doorway. "Mrs. Moore, can you take care of Lavenia so I can go to school?"

Mama turned to her. "Angie! What I tell you? Why you ask Mrs. Moore that?"

"It's all right." Mrs. Moore laughed. "Sure I can take her. You mean you want to go to school, Angie? That's new. What's goin on?"

Angie ran to get her book bag.

"Some new dance teacher or sumpum. Hand me that bottle bag, would you, Moore?"

"Here. I've never seen her so excited about school before."

Angela rushed into the bedroom, kissed her mother, thanked Mrs. Moore, and ran out of the apartment, down the three flights of stairs, out the stairway door into the lobby, and pushed open the outside door just as Michelle was about to ring her bell. "Stop," she yelled, "I'm here!" The two girls breathed deeply and pretended to faint against the walls but recovered quickly and hurried off giggling down the block to school.

"You got your paper?" Michelle gasped, wide-eyed.

"Yeah, it's in my book bag. Get it for me. Let me see yours."

Angie turned her back as Michelle gleefully unzipped the bag and took out the folded consent form. Then she turned her back and Angie took the precious form out of Michelle's bag. They hurried along Columbus Avenue. Just before reaching the schoolyard gate, Michelle stopped.

"What if Ms. Collier don't stay?"

"Don't stay?" Angie frowned.

"Yeah, remember the other acting teacher that came last year? She said she couldn't deal with us. She said the kids was animals and didn't come back. Remember?"

"Yeah, I remember. She sure did. Charlene and them was actin up all the time. What we gon do?"

"We gon be good, that's what we gon do. And I'm gon tell the kids to chill out so the teacher won't go. And they betta do it too."

"But suppose she don't like us anyway?"

"Angie, we gon be so good the teacher won't have no strength against us. We gon be good!"

"'Shell, maybe we can find her before she come to our class and look out for her."

"Yeah, that's right. Let's find her."

"She's probably in the principal's office."

Angie led the way through the crowded schoolyard and into the first-floor hall. From the doorway of the principal's office they looked in. Ms. Collier was there talking to the secretary. The girls waited.

"She got on some serious shoes," Michelle whispered.

"Yeah." Angie stood, bright-eyed. "Everything she got is serious."

All they could do was grin when she turned to leave and saw them watching her from the door. "Good morning, Ms. Collier." They said the words together.

Ms. Collier was pleased to see them. "Good morning, Angie and Michelle. Good to see you."

"Thank you." They blushed, backing out of the door. "What time you gon come to our class?" Angie asked.

Ms. Collier opened her folder and looked through her papers. "What grade are you in?"

"Five A," Angie and Michelle answered together.

"I'll come and pick you up." Ms. Collier spaced out the words, enjoying their suspense. "Oh, you're my last class."

"Your last class?" Angie and Michelle looked at each other, dejected. "We got to wait all that time?"

"I'm sorry," Ms. Collier sympathized. "Do you still want to come?"

"Yeah." Again Angie and Michelle spoke together. "We comin." They laughed.

"All right." Ms. Collier laughed with them but then waved her hand for them to be quiet. "See you later."

They covered their mouths, then ran and skipped to the stairway and up the stairs to their classroom.

After lunch Angie and Michelle were the first ones back to their classroom, and when the last period came and Ms. Collier and another Arts in Action teacher stood at the door, they led the cheers and applause that exploded in the room and annoyed Mrs. Cooper.

"We messed up," Angie whispered to Michelle. Mrs. Cooper stared at them, then slowly stood up and came around to the front of her desk where she folded her arms and stood. "Be quiet!" She pronounced the words firmly, crisply.

Michelle made a face and slid down in her chair. "We sorry, Mrs. Cooper," she sighed.

Ms. Collier and the other teacher waited at the door. Someone exhaled loudly. Someone else sighed and shuffled their feet. Finally Mrs. Cooper made a quick nod to Ms. Collier. The other Arts in Action teacher came into the room first.

"My name is Ms. Goddard. G-O-D-D-A-R-D." She spelled it out. "I teach music. Ms. Collier and I are from the Arts in Action program and we will come here to your school every Monday, Wednesday, and Friday. Those of you who have signed up for our classes, please line up in the hall when we call your names. If you did not sign up for our classes, please do not leave your seat. I am going to call the names of those who have signed up for my music class."

Mrs. Cooper raised her hand. "Take your belongings with you. You will be dismissed from your music and drama classes."

"Yes, Mrs. Cooper," the students droned.

"It's takin so long," Michelle complained quietly as the music students' names were called and they rushed to collect their books and book bags and then pushed into the hall, each one trying to be first in line. When the line was formed, Ms. Goddard led them down the hall to the stairway.

"I hope they don't do what they always do," Angie whispered.

"I told um to be cool." Michelle looked worried.

The classroom was still and quiet, waiting. No one looked at Mrs. Cooper or Ms. Collier. They were listening. Then it happened. When the music class reached the top of the stairs, they broke and ran as they always did when leaving class, laughing and yelling down the three flights of stairs to the first floor. Angie held her head and looked up to the ceiling. Michelle sighed and watched Ms. Collier. She was in silent eye contact with Mrs. Cooper, who continued to stand statuelike in front of her desk with her arms folded and now with raised eyebrows.

The other students in the class tried to keep serious faces as they heard Ms. Goddard's voice traveling up the stairs and down the hall and into their room, calling to her students, "Stop!"

Ms. Collier's face expressed pain and bewilderment, and Angie wondered if she were going to leave. But instead she walked to the center of the floor. "I am Ms. Collier. I am your drama and dance teacher. All those who have signed up for drama and dance, please line up in the hall when I call your name."

Angie and Michelle had put on their book bags and sat on the edge of their seats, waiting for their names to be called. Hector, Darrell, Cheryl, Pat, and Nia were among those students who signed up for the class. Even Charlene had changed her mind and signed up. Michelle stood next to Angie in line and whispered to as many students as she could, "Chill out. Let's be good so she won't go away like that other teacher."

They whispered their "OKs," "Yeahs," and "Unh huhs." When they reached the top of the stairway, Ms. Collier stopped them.

"I know you are not going to do what that other class did. Are you?"

"Nooo," the class assured her.

"Good. We are going to Room 118 on the first floor. Let's walk quietly and in an orderly way. Are you ready?"

"Yes." They repeated their assurances.

Ms. Collier turned and began to lead the students down the stairs. On the first landing, Hector broke the line and ran yelling past Ms. Collier. Darrell, Pat, Cheryl, Dawn, and Charlene did the same, dodging to avoid Ms. Collier's grasp and ignoring her plea for them to stop.

Only Angie, Michelle, Natilee, and Nia were left from the line. "We ain't never gon have nothin,'" Michelle protested, clumping down the stairs. They reached Room 118 just behind Ms. Collier. Hector was twisting and pulling the doorknob and banging on the door, but it was locked. The others were running in the hall, laughing and playing nervously, when Ms. Collier hurried up to them. Standing again in front of the few students who were in line, she spoke softly but firmly. "Get back in this line. Quiet down right now or I will take you back upstairs. You will not have a class."

"You all blew," Michelle criticized, pointing her finger at the offenders. "'Cause of you I bet she ain't comin back," she whispered. "We just gon be doin the same old thing."

Charlene walked past Ms. Collier and began beating on the door. "Open the door," she shouted. "Open this damn door! We don't care what you say, Michelle. You just tryin to kiss the teacher's ass. You so goody-goody."

"Stop that," Ms. Collier demanded again in a low voice, catching Charlene's arm and pushing her away from the door. "Go back in line."

Charlene jerked her arm away from Ms. Collier and stamped back into line. "Don't be pullin on me. You ain't my mama."

"Class," said Ms. Collier quietly, "you will not do again what you just did and stay part of this program. We can have a good time together learning new and exciting things, but I will put you out of this program if you refuse to be respectful to me, yourselves, and this class."

The students stood still and quiet, watching Ms. Collier's anger.

"That's how you are." Darrell scowled.

"Yes." Ms. Collier spoke quickly. "That's how I am, if this is the way you intend to be. I will not have it. You have a lot of energy but you must control it and do something good with it. Do you understand?"

Darrell looked away and Ms. Collier was answered by a chorus of sucked teeth and scattered, angry, and confused looks. Angie folded her hands on top of her head and leaned against the wall. Michelle stood with arms folded, watching Ms. Collier. Finally everyone was quiet.

"When you go into the room, you will see a man. He is our drummer. Line up immediately so we can begin dancing. We have lost most of our class time."

Ms. Collier unlocked the door, slowly opened it, and the students, with Angie and Michelle at the end of the line, sullenly filed past her and into the room. They immediately erupted again, pushing each other, karate chopping, writing on the blackboard, and scooting around the floor in chairs. Now both Angie and Michelle leaned against the front blackboard with their arms folded. "This is the wack." Angie scrunched up her face.

Ms. Collier raised her hand and signaled to the drummer to come to the center of the room. "You lost control again, didn't you?" she asked the young students.

"They sure did," Michelle and Angie agreed.

Darrell and Hector followed the drummer to the center of the room, trying to touch his drum. He wouldn't let them touch it but told them to "Come on!" Angie and Michelle left the blackboard and stood together, forming the beginning of the first line. Natilee and Nia saw what they were doing and stood next to them. The drummer stood next to Ms. Collier. "You have lost control again, haven't you?" she repeated. "We have only ten minutes remaining in this class."

Finally Charlene stopped pushing chairs and with her arms folded stood next to Angie and directly in front of Ms. Collier and the drummer. The others followed her example, completing two lines across the room.

"If"—Ms. Collier spoke slowly—"when I come in on Wednesday, your behavior causes me to suspect that you are going to lose control of yourselves as most of you, the weak ones, did today, I will cancel your participation in this program and will leave you in your classroom. Only those who have strong characters can come to this class. You better get real if you want to be here. Now, who wants to be here? Don't say anything. Raise your hand if you want to come back to this class."

Angie and Michelle had their hands up first. One by one the other students raised their hands, all except Charlene, who was trying to stare Ms. Collier down. Finally she raised her hand quickly, then folded her arms again.

"OK." Ms. Collier nodded. "When you raised your hand, that was your contract. Your agreement that you will from now on in this class be of strong character. That's the agreement that we share. My character has to be just as strong as yours. If I break our agreement, I expect you to tell me about it, because I am sure going to tell you about yourselves if you break it. Now, this brother you see standing next to me, our drummer, is named Labri."

Brother Labri played a roll on the drum and the young people applauded and began to bounce in excitement. Angie and Michelle hugged. "Look at Ms. Collier, she smilin." Angie grinned. The drummer continued to play.

"Before we dance"—Ms. Collier's voice was

soothing now—"we have to give praise, thanks that we met each other and that we are going to learn something new. In many parts of Africa the people have a special way of giving praise. It's called ululation. Say that."

"Ululation!" the class shouted.

"All right!" Ms. Collier grinned. "Now, you do it like this." She opened her mouth and moved her tongue rapidly, making a high-pitched sound.

"I can do that." Michelle raised her hand just before Angie raised hers and said the same thing. The whole class wanted to do it.

"Are you ready?" Ms. Collier asked. "When I say 'Inhale,' you inhale. When I put my hands down like this, you let your breath out and ululate. Got it?"

"Yes," they shouted.

"All right, now let me see you do it."

Ms. Collier raised her hands but suddenly Charlene lurched to the side into Angie, almost knocking her down. She yelled at Angie, "What's wrong with you?"

Rushing at Charlene, Michelle yelled, "I saw you. This is payback time."

Ms. Collier stepped between them and held Michelle back. Michelle was furious. "She tryin to start sumpum again, Ms. Collier!"

Charlene's supporters were behind her, and Natilee and Nia were standing with Michelle and Angie. "She tryin to keep it goin." Angie spoke loudly and pulled Michelle away from the confrontation. "But we ain't gon pay her no mind. We gon dance and act. That's what we came here for."

"You shut up, ugly!" Charlene leaned around Ms.

Collier and hollered the words at Angie. "What you buttin in for, Michelle? I wasn't talkin to you!"

"We really gon kick yo ass this time." Cheryl pointed at Angie. "Blacky! Slave!"

It had all happened so quickly. Ms. Collier looked at the drummer. For a minute they couldn't believe what was happening. Then Mr. Labri began to open the small crowd and stand each child in line again. "Didn't you agree to keep control of yourselves? Where is your self-control? Turn around, young sister, and get in line. Right now!"

Charlene continued to glare at Angela and Michelle. "You not my sisters!"

"She not listenin, Ms. Collier," Michelle warned.

"Let's start our ululation again. I'll do it for you first." Again Ms. Collier made the sound of praise. "First breathe in deeply. Then let your breath out as you ululate, when I let my hands down. And"—Ms. Collier raised her hand—"breathe in."

"This old mess ain't nothin," Charlene shouted. "I ain't gon do it. I ain't no African. I ain't no bugga bugga."

Charlene's gang laughed with her.

"Sumpum wrong with that girl." Angie shook her head.

"Nothin ain't wrong with me. Sumpum's wrong with you, Blacky!" Charlene screamed.

"What is your name?" Ms. Collier asked.

"Charlene! Charlene!" Angie's group answered.

"Shut up!" Charlene yelled at them. "I can say my own name."

"Oh yes, Charlene. I'm going to give you a note,

85

Charlene. You don't need to be in this class." Ms. Collier opened the folder on the desk. "Take this note to Mrs. Cooper."

Charlene pushed Ms. Collier's hand away from her. "I ain't goin nowhere."

With one step, Angie moved past Ms. Collier and stood facing Charlene. Surprised, but not wanting to show fear, Charlene slowly stepped back from her. She had only meant to make Cheryl and Pat think she wasn't afraid of Angie after what happened in the fight. She was just selling wolf tickets. But Angie had bought them. And Charlene saw the same look on her face that had been there when they were fighting and Angie had her down on her back in the street. Charlene stared wide-eyed at Angie. Angie stared back.

"I come here to learn me sumpum." Angie spoke slowly, her voice almost a hiss. "How come you always have to argue and fight? Can't you just do what the teacher say sometimes? And shut up yo mouth? I got me a task to do. I got me some people I gotta help. I am gonna get me some knowledge and I am not gonna let you mess up this class."

"You always tryin to be so different," Charlene shouted. "Actin like you betta than everybody else."

"We can't be fightin and playin all the time," Angie shouted back. "That's borin. I'm not trying to be betta than nobody. But my mama and my daddy and my Great Cousin Seatta told me to do my best and that's what I'm gonna do. So you betta chill and listen to what the teacher say, 'cause if you don't, even if I am scared, if you start sumpum, little scared ugly Angie gonna stop it. Now, make yo move."

Without breaking the stare, Charlene stepped back. Angie stepped with her. Ms. Collier and Brother Labri watched everyone.

Charlene swallowed. She was perspiring and the only sound heard in the room was her breathing. Angie coolly returned her stare. In one quick movement, Charlene folded her arms and looked down at the floor, away from Angie. She walked slowly to the back of the room and said quietly over her shoulder, "This ain't nothin."

"All right," Ms. Collier said softly. "I think we are back in control now. Let's start the class."

The bell rang.

Chapter Five

Wednesday morning, before they went to class, Angie and Michelle walked into the principal's office and sat down on the bench just inside the door. After watching them a while, the secretary asked, "Are you two waiting for the principal?"

"Who?" Angie and Michelle looked at each other. "The principal? No, we waitin for Ms. Collier. Did she come in yet?"

"No," the secretary answered, "I haven't seen her yet."

"Did she quit?" Angie asked.

"I don't know. I don't think so." The secretary looked at them, frowning. "Can someone else help you?"

"No, we just wanna see Ms. Collier." Michelle smiled.

"Who wants to see me?"

Angie and Michelle felt caught. They hadn't intended for Ms. Collier to see them. If she hadn't quit, they thought she would come in through the door near the time clock on the other side of the room, but she came in the door next to where they were sitting, and there she stood, looking at them. They both stood up at the same time. "Good morning, Ms. Collier," they sang out.

"Good morning," she said, smiling. "You want to see me about something?"

"We just wanted to see if you was coming back." Michelle grinned as she and Angie circled Ms. Collier and waved as they hurried past her and out of the door she had come in.

"I told you she was comin back," Michelle bragged as they rushed up the stairs.

"Yeah. Did you see those big boxes she had?"

"Yeah, she got sumpum for us."

"I'm gon tell everybody she got sumpum for us. Everybody but Charlene." Angie laughed.

Later, in the lunchroom, the younger students who had Ms. Collier's class earlier in the day told Angie and Michelle, "She said it was sumpum for you. For the 5A class. She said we too young."

"It's just for our class?" Angie and Michelle were thrilled.

When lunch was finished and they were back in class, Angie and Michelle spread the word about Ms. Collier's surprise. "It's just for us," they bragged. And when Ms. Collier came to get them and told them to go on ahead in the hall, the line formed quickly and moved to the top of the stairway with Angie and Michelle leading the way. They stopped the line there and waited for Ms. Collier to come to the front. "Be cool," Michelle whispered. No one moved or broke the line or laughed or screamed. They waited and watched Ms. Collier and she watched them, holding her breath, delighted when one of them asked, "You got sumpum for us?" And especially when Charlene asked, "You like us, Ms. Collier?"

The line descended without a shout or a shove. As they approached Ms. Collier's room, Charlene lost faith. "We ain't gon do nothin special," she warned. "Just wait and see." This time her warning was answered by a chorus of sucked teeth, and rolled eyes and grins from Angie and Michelle. When the door was opened, the double line of children surged forward into the room. They stopped in the center. Their eyes wide, they turned in circles to see the surprise.

"Isn't it grand?" Angie sang the words, spacing them.

Lengths of red, brown, yellow, purple, and mixed-color fabrics stretched from the ceiling of the room, crossed in front of the windows, and dropped onto carved Ghanaian stools set in opposite corners. Calabash bowls, feathered fans, brass and iron bracelets, anklets, and earrings covered the table. Long cowrie-shell collars, beaded veils, and elephant tail whisks hung from the top of the blackboard; gold and silver lace, grand Buba gowns tacked in place, were spread out and glistening, hiding the wooden sliding-door cabinet. The soft gourd and metal music of the African Kalimba flowed from the tape machine hidden beneath the table, and the scent of incense filled the room, changing it into an exciting place of new sounds, scents, colors, and shapes. Ms. Collier had overdressed and in the corner of the room quickly took off her long overgarment, and as the Kalimba music changed to drum rhythms, the children turned to see the golden fabric of a grand Buba gown billow around Ms. Collier as she whirled and stretched and bent, dancing toward them.

The class "Yayed" and clapped and formed a circle around her, some ululating in their delight. Angie couldn't believe what was happening. The classroom was now like her dreaming room when she got the golden shimmershine feeling. And just as she always danced in her dreaming room, Angie stepped into the dancing circle with Ms. Collier and danced. As she moved, the brilliant colors that draped the room, the young faces, the carved and woven shapes, all blurred around her. Only Ms. Collier was clear, and Angie mirrored her movements, turning, jumping, twisting when she did. The class was stunned and whooped their delight. Even Charlene and her gang were impressed. This was not the scaredy-cat Angie they knew. This was a new Angie and she could dance.

Michelle led the squeals of delight and the applause when the dance ended. Angie looked at Ms. Collier, thinking maybe she had done wrong to dance with her. Ms. Collier saw the question and the fear. "It's all right, Angie. We're happy that you danced. You were great. Wasn't she, class?"

With barely a smile, Angie watched her classmates applaud her, even Charlene, Cheryl, and Pat. Angie felt strange and she didn't understand the feeling. "You got the shimmershine," Michelle whispered in her ear.

"Yeah." Angie finally smiled. But it wasn't just the shimmershine. Something else was happening.

"All right, class." Ms. Collier waved her hands, directing them to bring their chairs into a semicircle around her. "I have something to ask you. Would you like"—Ms. Collier sat down on her tall stool—"to do a play?"

"Yes," the class answered. Angie and Michelle exchanged smiles but Angie was still in her shimmershine dream world.

"The play," Ms. Collier explained, "starts in Africa, then moves to America. The beautiful clothes, fabric, and jewelry you see all around come from Africa and are part of what you will wear in the play."

"Yeah!" the class responded.

"What's in the box?" Hector stood up and asked. "You got sumpum else for us?"

"Let us see what you got," others asked.

Ms. Collier opened the box that she had placed on her desk. From the box she lifted a pair of children's-size pants, a shirt, and a dress. They were drab and torn and made of coarse cloth.

"What's that?" Charlene scowled.

"They are not beautiful, are they? Not something you would like to wear."

"No," the class moaned, and frowned.

"They all raggedy," Darrell observed. "They got holes in um."

Angie stared at the sad clothing. Great Cousin Seatta's words came to her. "Some didn't have no shoes and day clothes was raggedy." "Ms. Collier"—Angie raised her hand—"I think I know what they are."

"Good. What do you think they are, Angie?"

Angie's voice was almost a whisper when she answered, "I think they slave children's clothes."

"Ooooh! Slave children's clothes," Cheryl moaned.

"We got to be slaves in the play?" She sucked her teeth and slouched in her chair.

Hector stood up abruptly. "Not me! I'm not gon do the play if I have to be a slave."

"You don't understand," Angie explained to the class. "They was like us."

"Oooh, no, they wasn't like us neither. They was Africans."

"Let me tell you the story of the play. Then you tell me if you want to do it. Is that agreeable?"

Angie's "Yes" was louder than the rest as she sat forward in her chair to hear the story. The class became quiet, watching, listening.

"The play is called *The Dancing Children of Ghana*. The story begins in the seventeen hundreds, in Agogo, an Asante village in Ghana, West Africa. God had blessed the village with many children and, like all children, they loved to learn things and to play games. Some of the boys worked the bellows to fan a breeze for the Egofoo, the goldsmith, when he cast his metal jewelry and collected wood for the food fires. The girls helped the older women pound yam, care for the babies, keep the village clean, and make pottery. Most of all, the children loved two things. The first was to dance. Especially a dance called the Adewa. Whenever they heard the drummers playing Adewa, they would run to where the drummers were, where the villagers were gathering, and watch the adults dance. The children imitated their movements. They especially loved the hand movements that meant different things. One movement meant 'Let us unite.' Others meant 'We are strong,' and 'We are the best.' 'We are warriors,' or

94

'Whatever you do, enemy, we will get our way.' The children imitated the proud style of the dancers, the way the men wrapped their beautiful Kente cloth around them and stamped their feet to show their power over their enemy. The girls squinched their eyes when they danced, the way the adults did, to show disrespect and insult. And they touched their fists one on top of the other to show 'I have the power.'

"The second thing they loved to do was to draw proverb pictures in the loose soil under the large tree in the center of the village. One child would draw a picture of the two alligators with one stomach. One of the other children would have to guess what it meant."

"What did it mean?" Angie asked.

"It means 'We share life. We must have unity,'" Ms. Collier answered. "Then someone drew the picture of the bird that looks backwards, the Sankofa."

"What that mean?" asked Charlene.

"It means 'You can always correct what went wrong. Return and fetch what is yours.' If you couldn't tell what the proverb pictures meant, you were out of the game.

"Now comes the serious part." Ms. Collier spaced out her words. "One day, during the festival season, when everyone was praying, dancing, singing, and telling and listening to their history, from the surrounding forest European slave traders very quietly sneaked into the village and then attacked the people. With clubs the traders knocked them out. With long firesticks they shot some of the men. Everyone was tied up, even the children. Then they were made to walk for miles and miles to the coast. There the children were separated from the people of their village and put onto a ship that brought them to America, to a plantation in Alabama.

"They met other African people there. Many were Asante. All the African people took care of them as much as they could, but their lives were miserable and sad. The children saw that so many were whipped. So many cried and died. They were heartbroken.

"The slave makers did not allow the Africans to dance the way they did at home. They could only do simple dance movements that made the slave makers laugh. The children wanted to do something to help their new families. So, when they carried water to them in the fields in the afternoons, they drew proverb pictures in the soil in the rows between the cotton or corn plants—the two alligators with one stomach, the bird looking backwards, the ladder that leads from one life to a better one. When the grown-ups saw the drawings, it gave them hope, and they smiled at the children. But what made them laugh was when the slave makers made the Africans come to the fancy house where they lived, to entertain their guests. The Africans were made to stand together in the front yard and sing the new songs they had composed. After that, the slave makers always announced a special treat. The children were told to come forward and dance their 'funny little dance.' And you know what they danced?"

"The Adewa dance," Darrell answered.

"Yes, they danced Adewa. They squinched their eyes in ridicule. Stamped their feet in defiance. And with their dance movements, right in front of the evil slaveholders, they said, 'We are warriors, we are powerful, you will never defeat us. Whatever you do, enemy, we will get our way.' The slave makers laughed and laughed and applauded the children. The Africans smiled lovingly, but all night in their cabins they laughed and celebrated what the children had said with their hands and eyes and feet, with their Adewa dance.

"One day, when the children came to the field to bring water, an old man and woman whispered something to them. And then, when they carried the water down each aisle, the children drew a new proverb picture in the soil. It was the picture of the porcupine, the symbol of battle, of rebellion. The next morning, when the overseer rang the bell for the Africans to get up and go to labor in the fields, no one came out of the cabins. They were empty. All the Africans, including the dancing children, were gone. Some Africans on a nearby plantation said they had seen them flying over the fields that night, going home to Africa. Someone else said they had slipped over the state lines into Florida to live way back up in the swamps with other Africans and Indians. Wherever they were, the Africans were free and the dancing children had helped them get their freedom."

"Yay!" the class applauded. Michelle stood up and led it.

"You want to do it?" Ms. Collier asked.

Again the class cheered and applauded.

"All right." Ms. Collier rubbed her hands together. "I thought you would like it, so I already assigned you parts. I have scripts for you, with your names on them, and the part you play marked. In our play, An-

gie has the part of Akosua, the child born on Sunday.
Angie, you are our storyteller.''

"Me?" Angie asked, pointing to herself.

"Yes, you.''

Angie was shocked and turned to look at Michelle,
who was staring at Ms. Collier, waiting to hear about
her part.

"Charlene is Adjoa, born on Monday
Cheryl is Abena, born on Tuesday
Pat is Akua, born on Wednesday
Natilee is Yaa, born on Thursday
Dawn is Afua, born on Friday
Michelle is Amma, born on Saturday.
And Nia is our stage manager.''

"What's that?" Nia asked.

"I'll tell you. Now the boys.
Darrell is Kwasi, born on Sunday
Hector is Kojo, born on Monday.

And because we only have two boys in our class, I
am borrowing five boys from the other school where I
teach when I'm not here. They won't be able to come
before the day of the performance, but they already
know the dances because we were working at their
school before we came to work with you. I am very
pleased that you want to do the play. But, as I said, the
Arts in Action program started late in this school, and
we only have a short time to work on it before the
performance.''

"That's all right, Ms. Collier," Michelle assured her.
"We won't mess up.''

"We only have six rehearsals.''

"What we gonna wear?" Charlene stood up to ask.

"If I'm gonna dance and act, I have to look good." She put her hands on her hips and styled. Michelle looked at Angie with big eyes, but Angie didn't look back.

"Angie." Michelle touched her arm. "What's the matter?"

Angie didn't answer.

"You gonna look bad." Ms. Collier posed like Charlene.

"Do it, Ms. Collier!" Cheryl laughed and jumped up to pose alongside Charlene. Darrell and Hector whistled.

"I'm going to give you two things to take home. Those of you who have someone at home who can sew, raise your hands. I will give you some fabric and a drawing of the slave costume. It is very simple. The second thing I will give each of you is your script. Read it over carefully. Bring it back to our next class. Treat it nicely." Ms. Collier had walked to the table as she talked. The students were gathered around her and "oohed" and "aahed" when she showed them their African wraps and head ties. The room was noisy with their delight and excitement.

Angie and Michelle stood next to Ms. Collier. Angie still had the feeling of being in her dreaming room and she wanted to tell Ms. Collier how she felt, about Great Cousin Seatta, about the get-up gift, the shimmershine. She wanted to tell her about her mother's depression and about Daddy not being home anymore, about how maybe sometimes she would miss class because of taking care of her two little sisters. She wanted to tell her . . . "Ms. Collier!" Angie pulled on her arm.

"Yes, sweetheart?" Ms. Collier turned to Angie. "I have some fabric for you. Here it is. Does your mother sew?"

Angie nodded her head but didn't move to take the fabric or the drawing. Ms. Collier's smile slowly faded. "Is something wrong? You have a problem?" Angie stared at her, holding on to her arm.

Michelle took Angie's fabric and drawing from Ms. Collier. "She OK," she told her. "Sometimes Angie can't say nothin when she get upset. You have to wait a while. Then she can talk."

"Really?" Ms. Collier touched Angie's braided hair. "Well, Angie, you just take your time. Look at this beautiful braiding. I wish I could braid like this. You do this, Angie?"

"She not ready yet." Michelle continued to explain. "My mother braided it. She teachin me and Angie. My grandmama don't like it though."

"You gon help us with the words?" Cheryl interrupted. "With the readin?"

"Yes." Ms. Collier turned her head to look at Cheryl.

"These is real pretty." Cheryl reached up to touch Ms. Collier's earrings.

"You gon help me with my readin too?" Charlene asked as she looked at Angie holding on to Ms. Collier's arm. "How come you don't let go her arm so she can talk to somebody else 'sides you?"

Angie didn't look at Charlene, but Michelle glared.

"Listen, everyone!" Ms. Collier put her other arm around Charlene, who folded her arms and grinned at Angie and Michelle. "Anyone who needs help with reading come to see me next Monday at twelve-thirty. OK, there's the bell. Good-bye, see you next week."

"What kinda dance we gon do?" someone asked.

"You'll find out next week. Good-bye."

"How come they ain't goin?" Charlene asked, looking Angie and Michelle up and down.

"Out, Cheryl. They're coming too. I'm going to put them out in a minute."

When the students had all gone from the room, Ms. Collier told Angie and Michelle, "Come over to the mirror."

Angie felt better now. She let go of Ms. Collier's arm and, as they walked to the mirror, she took her fabric and drawing from Michelle. She didn't go close to the mirror but leaned against the blackboard, holding her things. Ms. Collier wrapped Michelle in the colorful cloth and tied her headpiece in place.

"Look at me, I'm gorgeous." Michelle sang out the words. "Look, Angie. Come get what you're gonna wear." Michelle began to dance around the room. Angie stayed where she was.

"My mama get sick sometimes." Angie finally began to speak. "Sometimes I have to stay home from school and take care of my baby sisters and I might mess up the play." She looked down at the floor and slid her back against the blackboard as she spoke.

"I'm sorry, Angie. I hope it's not serious. I hope she gets well soon."

"She just gets depressed sometimes."

Ms. Collier took Angie's hand and led her to the mirror. "You come when you can. Now, let us see

101

how you look in this." She began to wrap an amber cloth around Angie and roll it over tight at the top. "You want me to call your mother? Sometimes, when people get depressed, they feel better when they talk to someone about what's on their mind."

Although she was standing in front of the mirror, Angie did not look at herself in it. "Yeah," she said quietly, "she need to talk to somebody."

"Look at yourself. We gon be stars." Michelle put her arm around Angie's shoulder and smiled into the mirror. "We gon look just like twins. Look."

Angie looked at their reflection in the mirror, then looked away. "We don't look like no twins. You not as dark as me. Is she, Ms. Collier?"

Ms. Collier positioned them shoulder to shoulder. "Let me see. Michelle is a real nice dark brown with a little yellow and Angie is a real pretty dark brown with a little red. Just beautiful."

Angie looked straight at Ms. Collier. "Why you want me to be the storyteller in the play?"

"Because I think it will be good for you to speak in front of an audience and because I think you will do it well." Ms. Collier looked straight back at Angie.

"I won't look funny?"

"No."

"We look good, girl," Michelle bragged again in front of the mirror. "We are too fresh."

"I look different." Angie looked at herself.

Ms. Collier put her hands on her hips and styled in front of the mirror. "Angie, I think you look like me, and I think I am too fine, so I don't know what you are talking about."

"Ooh, Ms. Collier, you sumpum else." Angie and Michelle looked at each other and laughed.

"You numbers better 'sumpum else' on home. Go! I'm tired."

"Yeah, we betta go. We can't look at ourselves no more, we too gorgeous. We the shimmershine queens."

"The what?"

Angie and Michelle began to giggle. They collapsed on the table, burying their heads in the fabric.

"Come on, before you go, you have to tell me about the—what? Shimmershine queens?"

"That's the name my Great Cousin Seatta gave it. You know, like when you do sumpum good and you feel warm and shiny all over your body. That's the shimmershine."

"So you two are the shimmershine queens?"

Angie and Michelle helped Ms. Collier hang the remaining fabric and clothing in the cabinet. "We gon write a rap poem about it." Angie grinned, picking up her book bag and putting her fabric and drawing in it.

"Can you help us?" Michelle mirrored Angie's grin as she backed toward the door, her book bag on her back.

"Don't you two think I have enough work?" Ms. Collier collapsed into her chair at the desk. "Goodbye."

"Just a little bit?" Michelle pleaded from the door, with Angie looking over her shoulder.

"A little bit. Good-bye."

Angie and Michelle ran out into the schoolyard, making the ululation sound, startling the children still playing in the yard. They strutted and skipped down the street toward Columbus Avenue.

"I like Ms. Collier, don't you?"

"Yes, I think she gon stay."

That night Michelle's mother and grandmother came over for dinner and brought some hot meat patties that lived up to their name.

"Uh oh, you all used to um. One's enough for me." Mama laughed, fanned her mouth, and took a drink of water. "They just light you up."

"The last time Mama laughed so much, Daddy was here," Angie thought, watching her. She and Michelle had eaten as many hot patties as they could, with Angie making tongue-sticking-out faces, drinking water to cool off, and leaning back in her chair with her mouth open, panting for air. Michelle's mother and grandmother laughed at them and congratulated Mama and Angie on the rest of the meal.

When the conversation turned to the play Angie and Michelle were going to do, everyone was pleased except Grandmama. "We got more Indian than African, you hear me?" She leaned forward, looking everyone straight in the face. "My grandfather was Indian, come over straight from India. I can't see why the school pressin African on the children, and slavery. I can't see how it so. That's past. And putting the braids in the children's hair. I tell you, we got Indian. And don't be cutting ya eyes at me, Angie and Michelle. Both of you got good hair. Why you braid it so? You born here, not Africa."

"Mama," Michelle's mother sighed. "Mama, all of

us have good African hair. For a long time we've been tryin to change it. We have pulled it straight with hot pullers, ironed it on ironing boards, fried it and burned it with straightening combs and lye. We have blown it out and pressed it flat, but our hair got more sense than we got. Our hair keeps goin home, goin home, our hair keeps goin home. Africa keeps claimin us, hair an all, Mama. And it's all right."

"Oooh." Angie's mother reared back in her chair, laughing. Angie watched her, wishing even more that Daddy was there. "I'm glad you all came over for dinner." She grinned at the guests.

Grandmama widened her eyes at her daughter. "The child know more than the mama?"

"We glad we came too. Right, Mama?" Michelle's mother touched her mother's hand.

"Unh huh." Grandmama gave in with a nod.

"It's a nice play," Angie informed the table. "Everybody got a good part in it. Mama, I'm gonna call Daddy and ask him if he can come see my play."

"That's a good idea." Mama nodded.

"Does the play have some Indians from India in it?" Grandmama asked.

"No, ma'am." Angie shook her head. "It's about some children in Ghana. Then they come to America. That's the slave part."

Grandmama sucked her teeth and began another hot patty. Angie and Michelle wanted to grin but made their faces blank, settling for opening big eyes at each other, sending the message "Let's go rehearse."

"We finish, Mama. We gon go rehearse now. Come on, 'Shell. 'Scuse us." Angie got up from the table and took her dish over to the sink. Michelle did the same. "Excuse me."

In the bedroom, Angie fell laughing across the bed, then sat up, feigning seriousness. "I don't wanna talk about your grandmama." She shook her head as she spaced out her words.

"Go 'head." Michelle flopped down next to Angie. "She always talking 'bout she Indian."

Suddenly Angie became serious. "Let's get our scripts." She bounced from the bed and quickly stepped to the small desk in the corner where she had put the scripts before dinner. Sitting cross-legged on the bed, she and Michelle opened their scripts.

"You got the biggest part." Michelle scrunched up her face.

"That's in the African part. In the slavery part you got more."

"Yeah."

"I gotta remember all this?" Angie rolled over on her side, pretending to faint. "This is impossible."

"But you gon do it, right?" Michelle challenged.

"You got that right." Angie sat up, serious again.

"Ooh, this is gon be great." Michelle bounced off the bed and began strutting around the room. "I stand up in front of the other kids and say, 'To help our new family feel better, let us dance Adewa!' All right!" Michelle posed with her hand on her hip.

"Then I say . . ." Angie stood up, looking at the wall as if it were an audience. "'The dancing children danced as they had danced back in their village. And the elders smiled with remembrance and pride. They felt even better, though it was only for a short time.'"

"All right." Michelle strutted again. "We gon be bad!"

When the nervousness and joy of their first real rehearsal had cooled, Angie and Michelle sat again on the bed and, from the beginning of the script, read the play, once, twice, then a third time, until they remembered nearly all their lines. They would have read it again had Michelle's mother not called, "Come on, Michelle, let's go home. It's gettin late."

Chapter Six

On Friday some of the students brought the shirts and pants their mothers had stitched over the weekend from the fabric Ms. Collier had given them to take home. All were eager to start rehearsals, and without being told they formed a semicircle of chairs around Ms. Collier's stool and sat down, anxious to begin.

Some of Ms. Collier's friends were there. They had come to play the adult parts. The children were excited by their presence and turned in their seats to admire and question the professional actors.

"Do you act on TV?" Angie asked.

"I think I saw you in that movie 'bout those computers and robots, right?" said Darrell.

When Ms. Collier finished pulling the window shades down and stood again in the center of the semicircle, the class turned to give their attention to her. "Before we read our scripts, I would like to show you some slides of the people whose story we will be telling in our play. Is that OK with you?" Ms. Collier moved her stool to the side of the room.

"Yes, Ms. Collier," the class answered.

Hector reached over to the wall and pushed the light switch, snapping the room into darkness just as Ms. Collier turned the slide projector on, brightening the screen that had been pulled down in front of the blackboard with a colorful projected image.

The class "oohed," wide-eyed with surprise and joy.

"The pictures were taken in Agogo. That's in Ghana, West Africa." Ms. Collier's voice filled the dark room. Michelle elbowed Angie in the side. "Look." But Angie was already looking and didn't even feel the nudge. "That girl on the screen look like you and Ms. Collier," Michelle whispered.

"Ain't nobody look like Angie," Charlene's voice drawled in the darkness.

"Nobody look like yo mama neither, Charlene," Michelle drawled back. "Nobody 'cept the wolfman."

Angie watched as a worried look came onto Ms. Collier's shadowed face, as she looked around the room for the reaction to the signifying that had just gone on. But the students let the remarks pass without taking their attention from the slide screen. Angie looked back at the slides as Ms. Collier began to describe them. "These are Asante people in Accra, the capital city of Ghana, West Africa."

"You been to Africa?" Pat asked.

"Yes, I have, several times. See the man being carried there in the slide. He has just been made king of the Asante people. They call it enstoolment. You can see some of the children on this slide, but let me change slides and you will see some children dancing Adewa."

"There they are!" Cheryl shouted. "They look beautiful. We gonna look like that?"

"Yes, Cheryl. Look at this slide. Thousands of people were there."

"Look at the men dancing. I'm gonna go there one day and dance," Darrell said.

"Yes, I hope so. Well, that's it. Turn on the lights, Hector. Let's start our reading."

Angie and Michelle smiled and rubbed their hands in anticipation. "Let's start," they chanted.

The class quickly opened their scripts to page one.

"Let's try to read the whole script without stopping, OK? Those of you who came to me for help at lunchtime today, how did we agree to read?"

"Slowly and clearly, sounding out the words," Charlene, Cheryl, and Darrell answered together.

"Right." Ms. Collier nodded at them. "Our storyteller, Angie, opens our play. Whenever you're ready, Angie." Ms. Collier sat down at her desk, then noticed that Angie was not responding. She sat with her head down. Her hands were folded on her script which lay open on her desk. "Angie," Ms. Collier continued to encourage with a smile. Darrell sighed and slid down in his chair.

It had happened so suddenly. Angie felt as if she were going to faint. She felt her heart beating. She could hear it. Her mouth was dry and she was breathing deeply. "Everybody gonna be lookin at me," she thought.

"Angie," Michelle called to her.

"Let me read her part, Ms. Collier." Cheryl raised her hand.

Ms. Collier shook her head. "Angie? You are our storyteller. Your first lines are right under the word 'storyteller.' Do you see them?"

Angie looked at her script but couldn't see the words clearly through the tears that filled her eyes.

"She can't read," Charlene yelled.

"Angie, come on," Michelle urged. "Wait a minute, Ms. Collier. She gon be all right."

Cheryl got up from her seat and stomped to the corner of the room near the door, where she folded her arms and glared at Angie. "She scared," she yelled. "She scared, Ms. Collier. She gon mess up our show. She gon make us look bad. Pick somebody else, Ms. Collier. Please. She makin me nervous."

The word "ugly" was about to come out of Cheryl's mouth, but the changed expression on Angie's face froze the thought and word where they were. Angie stood up slowly. "I'm not gonna let Mr. Fear set up housekeeping in me," she thought. Picking up her book, she cradled it in her left arm, placed her right index finger under the first word of her opening speech, and, in a low steady voice, began to read. "My name is Akosua. I was born in the village of Agogo, in Ghana, West Africa. I am the storyteller and it is my honor to tell you a story entitled 'The Dancing Children of Ghana.'" When she said the title, Angie's voice trailed off to a whisper. She stopped reading and looked at Ms. Collier. She heard Michelle's voice call her from behind: "Remember, shimmershine!"

Angie began again. At first her voice was weak, but she repeated the words until at last it was strong and clear. "A story entitled 'The Dancing Children of

Ghana.'" She felt the shimmershine begin to warm her. She heard Cheryl say, "I heard that. Well, let me sit down."

Angie listened to herself reading. She liked telling the story. She liked her voice. When she finished her introduction, she didn't want to stop. The class didn't want her to stop either, and when she was finished, no one rose immediately to read, not until Ms. Collier called, "Hector?"

Angie sat down as Hector slowly rose from his seat and haltingly read his part, sounding the alarm that the village was being attacked. When Angie read again, her voice was even stronger, her reading better. Ms. Collier watched the adult and the young actors as they listened to Angie read. "She has them," she thought.

Then it was Michelle's turn and she too had the shimmershine and read with energy and style, with her hand on her hip. One by one, the class stood up and each did their best. Ms. Collier wanted to ululate in praise but instead she put her hand over her heart and took a deep breath. "You are going to be marvelous," she whispered. "You are going to be something else."

After class, Ms. Collier congratulated everyone, especially Angie and Michelle. Angie was nervous again and was unaware of the effect her reading had had on her class. When the other students and the adult actors told her how good she had been, she was surprised. Michelle said it was the get-up gift that made Angie and her do so well.

When they came out of the classroom, Angie and Michelle saw Charlene, Cheryl, and Pat just outside the door, leaning against the wall, waiting for them.

"They betta not start nothin," Michelle whispered to Angie as they walked past them and down the hall. Charlene called out, "Hey, wait up."

Angie and Michelle looked at each other, then back at the three girls coming toward them.

"What happened to you?" Charlene asked.

"Yeah," the other two echoed her question.

Angie and Michelle were puzzled.

"Ya goin to actin school or sumpum? You good." Pat spaced out her words as she complimented them.

"When you said"—Cheryl stood her tallest, pretending to be Angie reading in class— "'I am Akosua. I was born in the village of . . . ah . . .'" She laughed at herself for forgetting the name of the village. "Whatever. I forgot that African name. I thought you was really her. Serious. You was really good. And Michelle, you was too fresh."

Angie and Michelle stared at them.

"We serious," Charlene explained. "We thought you was good. But if you don't wanna take our compliment . . ."

Michelle's face smiled but her eyes didn't. "Yeah, we take it."

"Thank you," Angie told them with a faint smile. "We didn't know you liked it, that's all. You was good too."

"Naw, we don't go to no school," Michelle explained. "We just practice a lot until we get the shimmershine. We practice every day."

Charlene, Cheryl, and Pat exchanged glances, then asked, "What's that? What's the shimmershine?"

"Like everybody did good in class today, right? So

everybody felt good, right? That's the shimmershine feeling. You get it when you do the best you can. You feel like you be shinin all over. Everybody get it."

"Everybody get it? We got it?" Pat asked, looking at Cheryl and Charlene.

"Yeah," Angie and Michelle answered together. Michelle was enjoying their interest and admiration. "We work hard. That's when you get it. We work hard."

"Let's clear the halls," a teacher directed them as she tried to get past them to go out the door.

The girls let the teacher through, then followed her out the door and into the schoolyard.

"Can we practice with you?" Cheryl asked.

Still surprised, Angie and Michelle again answered together, "Yeah."

Angie and Michelle were now in the center of the girls as they walked.

"Where you practice?" Pat asked.

"Sometimes we practice in my house," Angie answered.

"Sometimes we practice in mine," Michelle added. "We gon practice tonight at seven o'clock at my house. Why don't you ask for permission to come over?"

"What buildin you live in?" Cheryl asked.

"We live in 2492. I live on the seventh floor. Apartment 7G."

"My apartment is 4G," said Angie.

Cheryl again imitated the way Angie stood in class. "We gon get good like you."

"And we can practice in my house sometimes," Pat offered.

"In mine too." "In mine too." Charlene and Cheryl agreed, separating in the direction of their buildings. "See you later."

Angie and Michelle waved and walked up the sidewalk to their building. "You think they serious?" Angie asked.

"They saw our shimmershine, yeah." Michelle opened the front door.

"Yeah. We was smokin. That's why they like us now. We good."

"You think they gon come? Maybe they gon start sumpum."

"Yeah, they gon come. They wanna be good like us. If they start sumpum, I'm gonna deck um."

The elevator was working again. Angie pushed the button, then asked Michelle, "You remember all those things Ms. Collier said we have to learn before the show?"

"She said we only have three more rehearsal hours. Three more!" Michelle took a deep breath, then using her fingers to count them off, she began to repeat Ms. Collier's rules.

"One: Whatever language a person speaks, they should speak it well. If you speak Africanized English, speak it well. If you speak Americanized English, speak it well. Understand that each one has its value and place and must be equally respected. Two: If you believe who you are supposed to be in the play, you will believe what you say in the play, your dialogue or monologue. Three—" The elevator door opened and Angie stumbled inside as if under the weight of all Ms. Collier's directions.

Michelle ran into the elevator after her, determined to put more weight on her. As Angie pushed the button for the fourth floor with a very weak finger, Michelle, almost doubled over with giggles, continued to give Ms. Collier's directions. "Speak clearly. Say the whole word. Everyone, including the person in the back seat, must hear you clearly. Four: Do not drag your feet!"

The elevator door opened and Angie, gasping "Stop!", stumbled into the hall and toward her apartment door. Michelle held the elevator door open and leaned out. "Five!" she called to Angie.

"Wasn't no five," Angie called back. She unlocked the apartment door. "But that's all right. We gon know it all."

Michelle let go the elevator door and pushed the button for the seventh floor. "See you later," they called to each other at the same time.

Mama was lying down on the couch when Angie entered the apartment. "Hi, Angie," Mama greeted her.

"Hi, Mama." Angie kissed her mother. "Did Daddy call?"

"Not yet, baby."

"How you feel?" Angie dropped her book bag on the floor and sat down on the side of the couch.

"Pretty good. How's your play comin?"

"It's comin good. I was good today. I was scared, Mama, but I read my part. I mean, I read it! Everybody said I was good. Even the real actors. They some of Ms. Collier's friends. Ms. Collier said I was good. When I started reading, I was so scared. I thought somebody was gonna crack on me. Cheryl tried to start something but she stopped. Mama, how come sometimes you get scared and sometimes you don't?"

Mama laughed. "I don't know, baby."

"When I was scared, I thought about Cousin Seatta and I said inside, 'Mr. Fear, go away.' And I thought about the slave kids that couldn't go to school. Then I felt better."

"That's good, baby. What 'bout you homework? What did Mrs. Cooper say?"

"Fe-ew, we had a spelling test. I did all right. I passed. You think Daddy gonna call tonight?"

"He probably will."

"Can I go to Michelle's house to rehearse at seven o'clock? Her mama said it's all right. And, guess what? Charlene, that girl I had the fight with. And her friends. We was so good in class, they wanna come rehearse with us tonight."

"That girl that tried to beat you to death?" Mama asked, raising her head from the pillow.

"Uh huh. She changed. She not callin names like she used to. But they saw our shimmershine. That's why they wanna come."

"You sure?"

"Uh huh. They were serious. Can I go?"

"Yes."

"Mama, you think Daddy gonna come see my play?"

"He said he was gonna try. Didn't he tell you that?"

"Yes, ma'am. He better come. I'm gonna be so good."

Mama laughed. "I know you and Michelle gonna

show out. Don't know how we're gonna stand you after the play."

When the telephone rang, Angie squealed and sprang from the couch to answer it. "That's Daddy."

"Angie." Michelle's voice came over the phone.

"Aw, shoot. I thought you was my daddy. Mama said I can come. What?"

"Pat called from downstairs on the intercom. Said they can't come tonight. Said they can come tomorrow. Mama said we can rehearse in the community room downstairs 'cause it's free till one o'clock on Saturday. So I told Pat to tell everyone, not just them. Darrell and Hector too. She said OK."

"But we still gonna rehearse tonight, right?" Angie asked.

"Yeah, later."

Chapter Seven

On Monday afternoon at twelve-fifteen, Darrell rushed into the classroom, announcing, "No lunch today. No lunch." The girls were adjusting their costumes near the table by the window. "We ate ours. You the slow one," they answered. "Ms. Collier, our costumes keep fallin off."

"Be careful. Wrap them the way I told you but put a pin in them to make sure." Ms. Collier spoke without looking up from the cue sheet that she and Mr. Labri were studying.

"We goin to the bathroom to put on our costumes," Hector called back as he and Darrell left the room.

"Come right back," Ms. Collier called after them. Then, turning to the girls, "Let's line up so we can see what we look like."

The seven girls lined up across the room. Angie and Michelle stood shoulder to shoulder. "We got ours right," Michelle said as she checked her costume.

"Everyone has a headband," Ms. Collier said. Mr.

Labri checked his list. "Wrap? Necklaces? Good. Everyone has what they should have. Now hurry and change into your other costume. Mr. Labri will leave the room while you change."

Looking worried, Nia cautioned, "Don't let those boys come in here, Mr. Labri."

The slave clothes were checked and the process repeated with the boys. When that was finished and the clothing put away, Ms. Collier made an announcement. "It's time for your class. Thank you for coming here and giving up part of your lunch period. We had a good wardrobe rehearsal. I'll see you again at two-fifteen sharp."

The bell rang as soon as Ms. Collier finished speaking.

"We got one more rehearsal," Michelle said as she and Angie walked from the room and down the hall toward the staircase.

"One more day." Angie exhaled loudly. "And I've been speakin up and not lookin down, talkin up for myself."

"That's right. You been speakin up and not lookin down, talkin up for yourself." Michelle sang the words in rhythm and nodded at Angie. "My grandmama said she not comin, but I think she is. Your daddy comin?"

Angie began to climb two steps at a time, leaving Michelle behind her. "Yeah, he comin," she answered. Without looking back, she continued to the third floor and their homeroom.

"A lotta people gonna be there," Angie told her mother later that night, in the kitchen. "Sister Halima's workin with the principal. She the coordinator. She got the Black Studies committee to make up flyers and stuff for our show. And she said they been announcing our show on a children's program on the radio. Maybe Daddy heard it on the radio. I bet he said, 'My Angie's in that.'"

"Angie, if you don't wash the dishes, how am I gon dry them? Give me the dish, girl. Sister Halima always takes care of business. Is Michelle's grandmama comin?"

Angie laughed. "Michelle said she still fussin but she think so."

"Are you gonna wear your blue suit?"

"Uh huh. Michelle gonna wear her suit too. I wish Cousin Seatta could come. Let's see who's gonna be there from my family: Mama, Patrice, Lavenia . . ."

"Angie, don't ask me about your father again and don't be hintin."

Angie sighed. "I'm not, Mama. We got one last rehearsal Wednesday."

On Wednesday, the class rehearsed in the auditorium. They stayed for only a half hour because there was a dispute with the art teacher about who was supposed to be there. But the class was excited to be on the stage for even a short time, and between all else that was going on Angie managed to rehearse her entrance three times before they had to leave. When the rehearsal was over, the class surprised Ms. Collier with an ululation. Then Angie stretched out her arms and turned around in the center of the stage. "I got the shimmer shimmershine!" she sang out.

Michelle joined her, then the rest of the class, all turning in the center of the stage.

"Out!" a smiling Ms. Collier had to tell them. "See

you tomorrow, Thursday, at three o'clock sharp. We will rehearse in the gym until four o'clock. Then you go home and come back at six, and we do our show at seven. Will you remember that?"

"Yes, yes, Ms. Collier," the students answered as they left the auditorium.

Angie was quiet as she and Michelle walked home. Michelle knew she was worrying about her father coming. Just before Angie got off the elevator on her floor, Michelle told her, "Don't worry. He gon come."

When Angie closed the apartment door behind her, she looked around the room, expecting Mama to be there, but she wasn't. She was in the bedroom, sewing. Angie looked in, then walked over to the baby's bassinet in front of the window and tickled her. "Hi, Mama."

"Hey, baby." Mama didn't look at Angie. "How was school?"

"Fine. We had our last rehearsal."

"Was it a good one?"

"Uh huh."

"I know she's waitin for me to tell her her daddy called," Mama thought. "I pressed your suit and made you a new blouse from some material Cousin Seatta brought me. See? Isn't it pretty?"

"That's for me, Mama? It's beautiful. Thank you."

"Yes, it's for you. I don't have any other actress in my family. You're the star."

Angie kissed Mama on the cheek and held the new blouse up in front of her as she walked down the hall to her room. With great care she hung the blouse in her closet next to the suit her mother had pressed. Angie closed the closet door slowly, and just as slowly walked over to the bed and sat down. She felt tired. She sighed and let the straps of her book bag fall from her shoulders.

"He's not comin," she whispered. "He not never gonna come home."

New and different feelings were moving into Angie. Always before she had felt only love for her father, and, after he left, a longing for him to come back. But now anger tightened her jaw and set a coldness in her eyes. If Daddy didn't want her, she wouldn't want him. She would protect herself from the pain of caring for him.

"I don't want him either," she said. "He don't have to come see me. I don't need him no more. He don't mean nothin to me."

Again, Angie wouldn't let herself cry. The tears were there, but she blinked them back, swallowed, and sat in silent battle with her new feelings of anger and rejection and confusion. "How come him and Mama can't get along?" she asked. "Botha them make me tired."

"Angie," Mama called from her room, "I need something from the store."

Angie went to the store for her mother, helped her cook and wash dishes. Later, when she was doing her homework in her room, Mama came to the door. "Why you so quiet?"

"I don't know," Angie answered softly without looking up from her desk.

"I know you thinkin about your daddy." Mama

125

took a deep breath and exhaled slowly. She didn't come into the room but watched her daughter from the doorway. "You are growin up now, Angie. Things are not always goin to be the way you want them to be. As you grow up, that's one of the things you learn. You have to deal with that, and mopin around doesn't help you or anybody else."

Mama had spoken slowly. She had spaced her words, trying to reach Angie through her sadness. "Do you understand?" she finally asked when there was no response from Angie.

"Yes, ma'am," Angie sighed. "I understand."

Later that night, Angie woke up suddenly. At first she thought the sound she heard was her alarm clock ringing, and she reached out and pressed the turn-off button on its back. But the sound didn't stop. Then it wasn't there anymore but her mother's pleading voice was. "Wait a minute, Kenny. Wait. You don't have to bring her anything. She just wants to see you."

It wasn't the clock, it was the telephone. Angie realized, "Mama's talkin on the telephone." She inhaled sharply. "It's Daddy." She was fully awake now, listening, her body stiff. "What's he sayin?" She silently mouthed the words, impatient for the conversation to start again.

"You don't have to take her anywhere. She just wants to see you, Kenny. You can take her for a walk, talk to her. She thinks you don't love her, don't want her."

Angie held her breath, listening.

"How is she supposed to know that? How are we

126

supposed to know that? You left us, we didn't leave you. When are we goin to talk about that?"

"Daddy," Angie whispered. She cried quietly. Tears rolled slowly from the corners of her eyes and down into her ears.

"Yes, I got your money order. I'm doin the best I can, Kenny. She told you she's gonna be in a play at school tomorrow. Are you comin? Wait, wait, wait, don't tell me that again. You don't have to bring her anything, just you. She needs confidence in herself, Kenny. She needs to see you there. You need to talk to her. . . . I am, I am . . . Dammit, Kenny, I'm doin the best I can. When you comin home? When you comin home?"

Angie covered her face with her hands and wiped the tears from her eyes and ears. This time the silence was longer. She listened for the sound of the receiver being hung up. It was very faint. Then there was the sound of Mama crying. Angie listened in the darkness until she couldn't hear the crying anymore. Then she slept.

On Thursday morning Angie took her time eating her breakfast and just as much time washing her dish and putting it away. Mama had tried to make conversation but Angie didn't have much to say, so Mama stopped trying. When it was time to leave, Angie went to the window and waved to Michelle, then dropped her a note telling her not to wait because she would be late. She watched Michelle walk down the block and cross the street. Then Angie put on her book bag, kissed Mama, and left for school.

Angie didn't want to talk to anyone, not even Michelle. At lunchtime she told Michelle she had to go home for lunch. Instead, she went into the Woolworth's store that was cattycorner from her apartment building. She walked slowly from one aisle to the next, just looking at the perfumes, the birds and hamsters in their cages, the sneakers. She stopped at the makeup display and took a packaged lipstick off its hook. "This color is nice. How it look on me?" She held the package close to her face and looked in the mirror that was part of the display. She turned away quickly, took another tube of lipstick from its hook, and compared them. "I like um both. I'll get one for Michelle." The next aisle was candy, and Angie walked through it casually, looking from side to side. As she walked, she broke the cardboard covering on the tubes of lipstick, slipped the tubes from beneath the plastic bubble and into the pockets of her jacket. At the end of the aisle she pushed the torn and empty packages between two boxes of candy on the bottom shelf and picked up two candy bars from one of the boxes.

"Is that all?" the cashier asked when Angie gave her the candy and the money for it.

"Uh huh," Angie answered. She didn't look at the cashier but at the magazines on the rack in front of the counter.

Michelle was jumping double dutch in the schoolyard with Nia and Cheryl when Angie came back. She saw her, stopped, and ran to her. "Ya mama betta?"

"Come on." Angie smiled and walked past Michelle and down the walk to a bench. Michelle watched her for a second, then followed her to the bench and sat down. "Sumpum's wrong," she thought.

Angie opened the paper on one of the candy bars.

"Want some candy?" Michelle bit a piece off the bar. "I got sumpum for you." Angie smiled. "Sumpum beautiful." She took the two tubes of lipstick from her pockets and stood them on one of the wooden slats of the bench. "Which one you like?"

Michelle looked at the lipstick, then at Angie. "Where you get them from?" Angie put the remainder of the candy in her mouth and leaned back on the bench. "You don't like um? I like the real red one but you can have both of um if you want um."

Michelle looked away from Angie. "You know I can't wear lipstick yet. Your mama won't let you wear none either, and that lipstick cost about three dollars apiece. And I know you don't have no six dollars to spend on no lipstick, Angie." With their arms folded, both girls sat stiffly on the bench, looking straight ahead.

"How you know I don't have no money? I got plenty money. My daddy gave it to me. You know everything?" Angie's words were bitter and Michelle stared at her.

"Sumpum's wrong, Angie. You not actin right. I bet sumpum happened."

"What happened?" Angie stood up quickly and glared at Michelle.

"All day you didn't wanna talk to me," Michelle told her. "I saw you walkin behind me slow. We supposed to be best friends. The shimmershine queens. But you changin to sumpum else. Stealin and stuff. Sumpum happened."

"I got problems!" Angie shouted. "With my daddy. I just don't wanna talk to nobody."

129

"At least you gotta daddy, Angie. Yours is not dead like mine. Least you gotta daddy."

"Well, my daddy don't want me," Angie shouted and ran off into the school without waiting for Michelle.

At three o'clock that afternoon, the cast of "The Dancing Children of Ghana" assembled in the gym and began their final run-through rehearsal. Angie stood in the taped-off space representing stage right. Michelle and the rest of the cast were in the stage left space. The music class was rehearsing on the auditorium stage, and the sound of music came into the gym through the door that connected the two areas. In the center of the rehearsal area, Ms. Collier stood with her arms stretched out to either side of her. "I am the curtain. The curtain is closed. You are in place behind the curtain. The music class has just finished in front of the curtain. They are gone. Sister Halima introduces our play. The last thing she will say is the name of the play. That's your cue to start. Are you ready?"

"Yes," the class answered.

"All right. I am Sister Halima, giving you your cue." Ms. Collier waited for two breaths, then announced, "Sister women, brother men, we now present: 'The Dancing Children of Ghana.'" Angie started to walk into place in front of the imaginary curtain, but suddenly there was screaming in the hall and the sound of a scuffle at the door. Everyone looked in that direction, just as the Arts in Action music teacher's voice was heard calling, "Open the door."

Ms. Collier hurried to open the door, and when she

did, Ms. Goddard pushed the five boys from the other school who were to work with Ms. Collier's class on ahead of her into the gym.

"What's goin on?" Mr. Labri asked as he and the adult actors went out into the hall to see what the problem was and if they could do something about it.

"There are boys out there with baseball bats," Ms. Goddard shouted. "They tried to hit these boys! Claimed they did something to them!"

Angie walked slowly over to the bench near the stage door and sat down. Michelle watched her, then did the same.

"They did!" Darrell shouted, and Hector agreed as they recognized them. The five visiting boys stepped closer to Ms. Goddard.

"I knew somebody was gonna start sumpum to try to mess up our show," Michelle complained from the bench. "Huh, Angie?"

Angie didn't answer, just watched.

"What are you talking about?" Ms. Collier asked.

Darrell and Hector pointed at the boys. "Last month a lot of schools went to a game at the Felt Forum. They was there with some other boys and they tried to beat us up. Ya know yaw did it." Darrell stepped toward the boys, who retreated farther behind Ms. Goddard.

"It's over!" Ms. Collier declared. She waved her hands in front of her. "It is over!"

Suddenly the door leading from the stage opened and the baseball-bat-waving boys ran into the gym and straight at the visiting boys, who fled through the opposite door. They were followed by the security guard and Sister Halima, who rushed through the gym behind them.

"Students, sit down! Everyone sit down," Ms. Collier commanded, "until this is straightened out."

Angie and Michelle leaned back against the gym wall and folded their arms. Charlene stood defiantly where she was. "We ready for um, Ms. Collier," she said. "Tryin to mess up our show!"

"Thank you, Charlene, but you sit down. We'll take care of it."

After a while Mr. Labri and the other adult actors returned to the gym and secured the doors. "Everything is under control," he told Ms. Collier and the students.

The visiting boys were with him. Ms. Collier put her arms around two of the boys. "Come on, children, let's start again."

Angie and Michelle hurried into their off-stage places.

"I am Sister Halima again. I have just introduced the play. Angie, make your entrance."

Angie walked into place.

"Don't look down at the floor, Angie. Look straight ahead," Ms. Collier directed.

"Yes, ma'am." Angie stood stiffly, looking straight ahead.

"Say your lines, Angie."

When Angie didn't speak, Ms. Collier went to her. "Are you all right?"

"Uh huh," Angie answered. She kept her glance straight ahead, following Ms. Collier's direction. That was a relief. She didn't want to look at anybody, especially Ms. Collier and Michelle. She didn't understand why. "Michelle was right. I am changin. What am I gonna do?" She felt a hand on her shoulder. It was Ms. Collier.

"We're waiting for you, Angie."

Angie moved her shoulder away from Ms. Collier's touch. "I gotta go," she whispered and ran from the room.

Ms. Collier was surprised and stared after her for a second, then told Mr. Labri to continue the rehearsal and hurried out the door after Angie. Michelle was right behind her. They both looked up and down the hall. The bathroom? She wasn't there. Outside the school gate, Michelle looked up and down the block. No Angie. Michelle hurried toward Columbus Avenue. Angie was not on the block, and Michelle knew that she couldn't have gotten home that fast. Maybe she had gone to their bench in the park?

But Angie had run in the opposite direction, up Amsterdam Avenue. She had run three blocks before she stopped at a playground. She was breathing deeply as she grabbed the chains of one of the swings and lifted herself onto it, leaning backwards, pumping until the swing began to rise higher and higher. She closed her eyes and listened to the chain squeak and knock as it moved in its fasteners. She pumped harder and rose higher. When she opened her eyes, the swing was level with the steel crossbeam from which it swung. "I wish I could fly," Angie thought, looking at the blueness above her, all around her. The park, the people, the street below her seemed very far away. She thought of her friend Michelle, of the stolen lipstick she had offered her, of how mean she had been to her. "I wish I was like Michelle," she thought. "She know how to deal with stuff. What am I gonna do?" Angie stopped pumping the swing and sat thinking as it swung lower and closer to the ground until it barely moved. "Now everybody mad at me—Michelle, Ms. Collier. Oooh, when Mama find out she gon get worried and depressed again. On account of me. On account of Daddy."

Stepping from the swing, she walked to the playground exit, but stopped. Several men who had been sitting on one of the benches in the playground began to argue and two of them started to fight. Angie watched them. They frightened her but what she felt most was anger. "Stop it! Stop fightin. You crazy!" she yelled, then ran to the corner and across the block to Columbus Avenue. Again she stopped at the Woolworth's store and again selected some makeup, tore it from its package, put it in the sleeve of her sweatshirt and paid for a piece of candy at the cashier's desk.

When Angie came out of the store, Charlene, Cheryl, and Pat were standing on the corner waiting to cross the street. "Angie," they called and came running to her.

"Why you run out of school?" Cheryl asked, out of breath from the run and the excitement of finding Angie. "Everybody's looking for you, girl!" Charlene shook her head. "Ms. Collier is upset."

Angie carefully took the paper off the candy bar without looking at the girls. "I don't care," she said. "I'm not gonna do the play nohow."

The girls looked at Angie, then at one another. As

they were talking, a man stood inside Woolworth's door, watching them.

"What's wrong with you?" Charlene asked.

"Nothin's wrong with me." Angie glared at them. "You always talkin about sumpum's wrong with somebody. Sumpum's wrong with you. I don't care about the play and I don't care about none a y'all. You ugly."

The three girls stared at Angie. "You betta shut up. You crazy," Cheryl told her.

Angie looked them up and down, then turned to cross the street, but just as she turned to go, the man from the store who had slowly walked over to them grabbed her arm.

"This is the second time I saw you take something out of this store, young lady. Come on inside with me. You kids are driving me crazy. Come on."

Surprised, Angie looked up at the man and tried to say something, but couldn't.

"Ooooh," Charlene, Cheryl, and Pat said, wide-eyed. "You a thief!" they called after Angie as the man led her into the store. "Let's tell Ms. Collier," the girls agreed, then hurried back to the school.

On the way they met Michelle, who, when she didn't find Angie, had returned to the school to finish the rehearsal. They told her.

Michelle ran to the store. Through the window she saw Angie standing with a man in front of the manager's office. When Angie saw Michelle come into the store, she turned away. She wanted to run again but the man was still holding her sleeve.

"What's your phone number?" Michelle heard the

man ask Angie when she came over to where they were. "If you don't tell me your phone number so I can call your mother, I will call the police and have them come and arrest you, take you to some home," the manager threatened.

"Don't do that, Mister," Michelle pleaded. She gave Angie her book bag and jacket that she had left in the gym when she ran out. "She my best friend. She got some serious problems right now. You gotta help her, Mister. The worst thing you could do is call the police or sumpum. She just made a mistake. She ain't bad."

"Oh, you're her best friend? What's her phone number? You want me to call the police or her mama?"

"You can't call my mama," Angie spoke up. "She sick."

"You want me to call the police?" the man asked Angie and Michelle.

"No," they both answered.

"Well, you better give me some phone number. You kids been stealing us blind."

"Unh huh, not Angie and me," Michelle protested.

"Not me and Michelle, Mister," Angie assured the manager. "This is my first time doin it. And Michelle didn't do it. Leave her out of it. I did it and I can pay you back in two weeks, 'cause Mama said I can work sometimes packing groceries at the supermarket. So you don't have to tell. . . ."

Mama and Ms. Collier had just come in the store and were marching down the aisle toward the manager's office. Angie stared at them with her mouth open. Her knees began to wobble and she sat down heavily on the large cardboard box that was behind her. Michelle scrunched up her face and leaned back on the sneaker table. The manager had followed the direction of their eyes and saw the two women hurrying toward them. Ms. Collier had called Mama.

"I thought you said your mama was sick," he said to Angie, who now sat with her elbows on her knees, her head in her hands, and her face scrunched up, looking at the floor.

"What is the problem?" Angie heard Mama ask.

"Is this girl your daughter, lady?"

"Yes, I'm Mrs. Peterson."

"She stole makeup from this store, Mrs. Peterson. Twice today."

Mama was holding Lavenia by the hand and the baby on her hip. She looked at Angie. "Did you say twice?"

"Yes, ma'am. She came in here two times."

"May we talk to you over there?" Ms. Collier asked the manager. She pointed to the corner at the end of the manager's cubicle office, and there she, Mama, and the manager huddled to discuss the matter. With big eyes Angie and Michelle watched as Mama talked fast, Ms. Collier talked slowly, and the manager nodded.

When they were finished, Mama and Ms. Collier turned toward the door. "Come on, girl," Mama said, looking at Angie out of the side of her eyes as she passed her on her way out. Ms. Collier walked beside Angie with Michelle behind them as they hurried behind Mama.

"Angie, Charlene told me you said you are not going to do the show. Is that right?"

"Yes, ma'am," Angie sighed as she rushed to keep up with Mama.

"You know Nia is your understudy and, yes, she can do the part but, Angie, it would be a shame if you didn't do it. You have worked so hard and your acting and dancing are good."

Angie stared straight ahead.

When they were on the sidewalk in front of the store, Mama stopped. "Don't pay any attention to Angie, Ms. Collier. She is not to say if she not gon do the play. Are you grown, Angie? Since when? We have to talk. Ms. Collier, thank you for your concern. I will call you in a little while. Come on, girl." Mama shifted the baby to the other hip and Lavenia to the other hand and crossed the street. Michelle walked beside Angie. They looked at each other.

The elevator was broken again and they had to climb the stairs. Angie and Michelle took Lavenia's hands as they climbed. When Angie and Lavenia followed Mama down the hall to their apartment, Michelle watched from the stairway door. She wanted to say, "See you later," but didn't know if she should.

When the door was closed, Lavenia ran to the bathroom and Mama went to put the baby in her bed. Angie sat down on the couch. When Mama came back into the living room, Angie told her, "I'm sorry, Mama."

"Girl, you betta be sorry! Runnin out of school! Havin people lookin for you all over the place! Take off that book bag! And stealin! Twice!"

"I'm gon pay for it, Mama."

"You certainly will! You have not lost your mind

completely! You know"—Mama spaced out her words—"I am two minutes off your behind. You betta apologize! You betta pay for it! And talkin about you not gon do the play, as hard as Ms. Collier worked, and Michelle, and me and you? Everybody lookin forward to the play. Then you get grand and say you not gon do it!"

"Daddy's not lookin forward to it, Mama. He's not comin!"

Mama sat down on the couch. "Let me tell you something about that, young lady. 'Cause I know that's what's at the bottom of all this stealing and stuff. You think ya father don't love you. Well, in the first place, you wrong. He does love you. And in the second place, if he didn't, if I didn't, you can't be fallin down. It's hard but when you feel hurt and rejected, that's the time you have to stand up and show what you made of. You can't go crazy just because somebody hurt you. You gon be hurt a lot in life. Everybody is. Hurt is all around us. Confusion, fear, and madness is all around us. But you can't become a thief because you afraid and confused and hurt. When you feel that way, you have to hold on to your values, to the ways that respect people and this life we livin. Didn't your cousin Seatta tell you that? Just be still till you can figure it out and see your way clear. That's your task! That's what growin up is all about! And you can't decide that you are not gon do the play 'cause you upset! People are dependin on you! The only ones who can say if you do the play or not are me and your daddy. You still a child and we are responsible for you. We know what's good for you and what's not. That's our task. We can't give that to you. We are responsible people. Your great cousin Seatta is a responsible woman. That's why she talked to you the way she did. We come from responsible people on back. Now, if you can't be responsible, I don't know whose child you are. My child would do the play." Mama leaned back and folded her arms. "But I am not gon make you do it. I want to see what you made of. Yes, this is a testin time for you, Angie. I wanna see if you belong to this family. I thought you was a shimmershine queen." Mama shook her head. "But now I'm not so sure. You go in your room and think about it. Then you call Ms. Collier and tell her what you decided to do."

Angie sat still for a while after Mama had finished and gone into her bedroom. Then slowly she walked into her room and sat down on her bed. She thought about her father, his not coming. She thought about Michelle, how they had rehearsed in that room, and what a good friend she was. She thought about Mama. "She been feelin bad but she didn't give up and act mean." And Cousin Seatta, Great Cousin Seatta. Angie closed her eyes. She could hear her voice. "The get-up gift . . . you got it too . . . those sweet seein dreams . . . I call it the shimmershine . . . we women gotta lot to talk about . . . it ain't gon be easy."

Angie opened her eyes. "Growin up sure ain't easy." She went over to her desk and sat down. "I'm gon write a poem about that." She opened her poem book. It was almost full. On the last page she began to write, but then noticed the poem on the page just in front of it. "Oh, I forgot about this." It was the rap poem Ms.

Collier had helped her and Michelle to write. "Ms. Collier had made everything so beautiful," Angie thought, "even me." Angie read the poem.

> *If you find yourself*
> *in a bad situation*
> *you can't let the situation*
> *situate you*
> *or hand you a half stepping*
> *self estimation*
> *or say*
> *how far you can go*
> *what you can think, say or do*
> *just listen to the get-up gift inside you*
> *let it move you, teach you, guide you*
> *then you will do your best*
> *and stand up tall*
> *and shimmershine*

The school auditorium was noisy with the sound of laughter and talk and wooden seats being opened or closed as the crowds of people that filled the room sat down or got up.

Michelle's mother and grandmother sat in the first row of seats. Grandmama had kept three seats empty on her side in hopes that Angie would come and that her family would use the seats. Michelle's mother looked at her watch. "It's quarter to seven. They're late starting."

The auditorium slowly darkened. The principal and various teachers came onstage to make announcements. Then the show started. The art class had a display. Some teachers did a skit. Then the music class played three songs. When they were finished, Sister Halima, with her African robe flaring out about her, walked from the wings to introduce the play. "Hasn't this been a wonderful evening?" she asked the audience. "Isn't that right?" The audience applauded. "We are rich because of our children. Isn't that right?" The audience applauded again. "Here we are now, at another high point in our evening. Our play. It gives me great pleasure to introduce to you 'The Dancing Children of Ghana.'"

In the dark auditorium Michelle's grandmother felt and heard movement next to her, and looked around to see Angie's mother, Lavenia, the baby, and Angie's father take their seats. Behind the curtain to the left of the stage, Michelle raised her arms above her head as she looked across the stage. Angie was on the other side with her arms raised. Together they did the shimmershine.

CAMILLE YARBROUGH has been an actress, composer, and singer, as well as a writer and teacher. A member of both the New York and touring companies of *To Be Young, Gifted and Black*, the author has taught in Harlem schools and is currently Professor of African Dance and Diaspora in the African Studies Department of City College. She lives in New York City.

No one ever said family life was easy!

WHAT IT'S ALL ABOUT
by Norma Klein

For eleven-year-old Bernadette (please call her Bernie!), life is anything but normal. She lives in New York City with her Jewish mom and her grouchy, unemployed stepfather. Her real father is a Japanese-American who lives in California and has just remarried. Add to this one newly adopted four-year-old orphan from Vietnam and a half-sibling on the way, and it's easy to see why Bernie's life is so tough sometimes. When her dad asks her to come live with him, things seem even tougher. Bernie must decide what being a daughter (and a big sister!) really means to her. And, slowly but surely, she begins to understand just what having a family is all about.

"Sympathetic, witty, entertaining and surprisingly unforced...the novel rings true."
— *Washington Post*

"As usual, Klein's style is slick, the dialogue easygoing, and the characters real enough to stick around in a reader's mind for a while."
— *Booklist*

BULLSEYE BOOKS PUBLISHED BY ALFRED A. KNOPF